W9-ATY-380

24,056

Teen
F
WIL

Williams, Michael

The genuine half-
moon kid

DUE DATE   BRODART   10/95   15.99

DUE DATE			

DISCARDED

the genuine
HALF-MOON KID

also by Michael Williams

Crocodile Burning

Into the Valley

My Father and I

the genuine
HALF-MOON KID

michael williams

LODESTAR BOOKS

Dutton   New York

No character in this book is intended to represent any actual person; all the incidents of the story are entirely fictional in nature.

Copyright © 1994 by Michael Williams

All rights reserved. No part of this publication may be reproduced or transmitted in any form or by any means, electronic or mechanical, including photocopy, recording, or any information storage and retrieval system now known or to be invented, without permission in writing from the publisher, except by a reviewer who wishes to quote brief passages in connection with a review written for inclusion in a magazine, newspaper, or broadcast.

Library of Congress Cataloging-in-Publication Data
Williams, Michael, 1962–
    The genuine half-moon kid/Michael Williams.—1st American ed.
      p. cm.
    Summary: Amid the political and social upheaval of South Africa, seventeen-year-old Jason is confused about his place in the world and the turmoil in his broken family. But in a quest for the gift his dead grandfather has willed to him, he finds peace.
    ISBN 0-525-67470-5
    [1. Grandfathers—Fiction.   2. South Africa—Fiction.   3. Family problems—Fiction.]   I. Title.
PZ7.W66715Ge   1994
[Fic]—dc20   93-42267
                                                CIP
                                                AC

First published in the United States in 1994 by Lodestar Books, an affiliate of Dutton Children's Books, a division of Penguin Books USA Inc., 375 Hudson Street, New York, New York 10014

Published simultaneously in Canada by McClelland & Stewart, Toronto

Originally published in slightly altered form in South Africa in 1992 by Tafelberg Publishers Limited, 28 Wale Street, Cape Town, South Africa

Editor: Rosemary Brosnan   Designer: Richard Granald
Printed in the U.S.A.
ISBN: 0-525-67470-5
First American Edition
10 9 8 7 6 5 4 3 2 1

24,056

for the Great White Mother,
S.S. Universe,
and all who sailed with her
on the Fall Voyage '91

DEPARTURE

JAY WATSON WANTED TO BE A FISH. Not an ordinary fish, but a tropical one. A bright orange fish, with a diaphanous, flame-colored tail fringed with silver, fragile dorsal fins, and wispy gills illuminated by sunlight. He wanted to be light and cool and gliding through water. He did not want to be filled with anger.

Cool it, Jay-o! Mom's not worth getting so mad about.

Jay strode furiously down Station Road, head lowered against the fierce Cape wind, clenched fists thrust deep in his pockets. For once he was not aware of the mass of flaming red hair swirling about his eyes. In his rage he permitted it to tumble as it would.

The southeaster swept over Devil's Peak and down the mountain slopes, to batter the city below. Papers whipped off the street. Signboards rattled. Tempers flared.

No way, Dad! How do you always get into our arguments? You're halfway up the African continent with your motorbike between your legs and your new woman glued to your back. And I want to know—why? Why did you leave just before the old man died? You knew he didn't have long. Why before Chuck died?

Jay had promised himself he would indulge only once a week but had almost immediately broken his promise. Here he was again, even though he had submerged yesterday, heading for Bob Lo's house with one purpose in mind. Not that he saw anything wrong with what he did there, but he didn't want anyone to catch him doing it. Jay did not want to be linked with any of the eccentricity that would label him a true son of his father. It was bad enough that his red hair constantly reminded his mother of her missing husband.

He quickened his pace at the thought of the bubbling, the caressing, the coolness, the harmony, and the many miniature rainbows awaiting him. Already he could feel anger relaxing its hold on him.

Why should I feel guilty about it? If Bob Lo finds out, I'll tell him I'm conducting a scientific experiment. He'd like that.

Jay didn't know what summoned him to those cool tanks of rainbows and bubbles. When he thought about it logically he could find nothing wrong with his craving, but nevertheless it was a secret he preferred not to share.

He strode across Darien Square and headed for one of the three alleyways that ran off of it, but before he started up Fish Alley he paused outside one of the cottages. The name *BAM* was written boldly in large red letters on the garden wall. The window blinds were down, but he thought he could see someone inside bending over a cutting table. He leaned across the low wall to get a better look.

"I know who you're looking for, but she's not here."

Jay had not seen Levi Bam, who was sitting behind the slats of the garden gate looking up at him and holding a pair of heavy black cutting shears. The boy's face had little of the child in it: His black eyes stood out like coals against his pale skin and fine hair, hair so fair it was almost white. At the outer corner of his left eye was a dark bruise, swollen from the cheekbone and extended to the eyebrow above.

"She's not here. You promised you'd take me to the cemetery. You haven't yet. And it's Friday already," Levi said sternly. He stood up, pointing with the black shears at Jay.

"What happened to your face, Lee?" Jay asked, distracted by the idea that Jenny Bam might nevertheless be in the house.

Levi flinched at the question.

"I fell off the table," he said, quickly raising his hand to hide the bruise. Abruptly he turned, marched up the path, and paused in the open doorway of the house. He glanced back angrily at Jay, his thin arms pressed tightly to his sides.

"It's Friday. And you promised!"

He spoke quietly but with a vehemence that made Jay feel guilty.

The prospect of seeing Jenny Bam had taken Jay's mind off his troubles, but Levi's accusing eyes recalled the sting of his mother's attack. Angry frustration welled up in him again. He turned away from the Bam cottage and made for Fish Alley, his need intensifying as he approached the hatchery.

"I know you want to get a look at her," Levi shouted after Jay, who tugged at his hair, trying to smooth it down, but gave it up as useless in the wind. With a rude gesture over his shoulder, he entered the alleyway leading to Bob Lo's house.

At the end of Fish Alley stood a dilapidated two-story Victorian house, the home of Bob Lo, specialist in the breeding of tropical fish. The house gave the impression of an old man smiling without his false teeth. Tufts of weeds and patches of moss grew on the slate roof, and the clogged gutters—a crease on the old man's brow—sagged dangerously. Below, two sash windows looked out onto the overgrown garden, and wooden shutters dangled from their hinges.

To Jay, the house was a refuge from his mother, her boyfriend, his grandmother, school, approaching adulthood, the new South Africa—in fact, from pretty much everything else in his life.

A square metal plate, nailed crookedly to the wall of the house, bore the following words:

BOB LO'S T OPICAL FISH
EMPORIUM
SAT 10-5
CLOSED ON SUNDAYS

Long ago some humorist had scratched out the *r* in *Tropical*. Since then the hatchery was known to the residents of Observatory as Lo's Topical Fish.

The brick wall surrounding the yard of Bob Lo's house was topped by a tunnel of barbed wire; a corner section of the wall had the extra protection of broken glass cemented into its bricks. The large wrought-iron gate carried a row of spikes and was fastened with a heavy padlock. When Jay had questioned the extensive security, Bob Lo had answered that his topical fish were worth a lot of money and that the world was no longer a safe place.

"Bob!" Jay shouted, hoping that his employer had gone to the dam for the day's supply of algae.

There was no reply.

"Hey, Bob!" Jay shouted again, pressing the buzzer beside the gate. He waited long enough to be sure that his boss was not in the hatchery. Then he leaned through the bars of the gate and felt along the inside of the wall for the ledge where Bob left the key when he went out. He found the key, unlocked the gate, and crossed the yard to the front door. As he entered the front room he again called out for Bob, but the house was empty.

Great! Not a soul around. You've got the place to yourself, Jay-o. Watch the time, check the hatchery first, and then get to the water. I need this more than the other times. If Gran can swallow the family silver, I can make like a fish. It must be in the genes. Even old Gramps was a little round the bend. No use fighting what's in the genes.

5

Jay made his way through a passage cluttered with piles of encyclopedias, old water pipes, a collection of miniature underwater castles, and sheets of glass. He was used to the disorder of Bob Lo's house and paid no attention to his surroundings as he passed through the living room, crammed with the plastic furniture and porcelain figurines that had belonged to Bob Lo's late wife, to the kitchen, which smelled of soy sauce and barbecued spare ribs. He went through the kitchen door that led to the office at the back of the house.

In Bob Lo's office, a confusion of papers, microscopes, fish trays, nets, buckets of squirming fish feed, old lamp bulbs, knitting needles, books, and dissected fish lay everywhere.

Princess Moonlight, will you sing for me?
Hey diddly-dee.
Riding a rainbow in Oscar's land,
forgetting all about the spoon-swallowing Gran.

Except for the corner that had been assigned to Jay, the office looked like a fisherman's junk room. Nevertheless, this was the laboratory of Hyung-Lee Chek Tensing Lo, alias Bob Lo, innovator in the breeding techniques of the neon tetra, tropical fish expert, and respected scientist.

In Jay's corner of the room was a small, uncluttered table. On the table were an old Corona typewriter, a small lamp, a magnifying glass, and a pile of neatly typed fish statistics and prices. It was an unspoken agreement between master and assistant that the scientific chaos of the one should not overflow into the orderly space of the other.

Jay passed quickly through the office. In anticipation he could already feel the humidity of the hatchery drawing beads of sweat from his arms and neck. The muffled sound of ceaseless bubbling produced in him an unbearable excitement.

He swung open the metal door leading from the office

and stepped into the hatchery. It was a long, rectangular room with eight skylights throwing shafts of sunlight onto rows of fish tanks. Down the center of the room and along its sides were large cement troughs in which a variety of tropical fish swam. The troughs were divided into several sections, each fronted by a glass panel.

The troughs held colonies of crabs, forests of underwater ferns and plants, schools of hovering sea horses, various species of live bait, and—the joy of Bob Lo's life—Chinese goldfish.

It was a room of endless bubbling, of silvery shadowed water, and of miniature rainbows—ribbons of light, trapped in the corners of the glass tanks—that beckoned to Jay.

Jay walked slowly between the troughs, deciding which was to be his tank for the day. He greeted the snout-nosed elephant couple, swirled his hand among the bright darts of brilliant blue neon tetras, admired the elegant curves of the moonlight gourami's fins, and prodded at the tiger guppies with their tails of floating fire.

The air in the room was moist and warm, and beads of sweat slid down Jay's neck toward the hollow of his back. In this room there were no loud arguments, no southeasters, no traffic noises, no sounds other than water running over rocks. The ceaseless chortling and gurgling ran over and through Jay, until the bubbles entered his blood.

Jay was sure he was the only one who could hear the hatchery's harmony. In the perpetual movement of fish gliding through bubbles that rose to the surface of the water and imploded with minute sounds was a sublime music. This was accompanied by the constant, reassuring gurgle of the water pump and the humming of its motor. The hatchery's song was the flick of water as fish thrust against the currents and sunlight was transformed into singing rainbows, dispelling all other daytime city sounds.

Jay stopped and knelt in front of a tank of spotted tiger

fish, black angels, blue tetras, and flaming volcanic guppies. He leaned his forehead against the cool glass of the tank and stared into the watery world before him. A monkey-leaf plant swayed gently, and from among its delicate leaves a baby guppy perceived Jay's sea-green eyes and swam up to the glass to greet him.

The fish knew that Jay was watching them, for they moved with him from one corner of a tank to the next, always summoning him, with the gentle opening and shutting of their tiny mouths, to join them. He had the right credentials: His red hair would provide the requisite flaming fins, his freckles the distinctive mottled coloring, and his lanky frame the obligatory streamlines.

Jay gazed into the pin-prick, inky eyes of a black angel as it gently nudged at the glass. Join us, it seemed to say, with an almost imperceptible flick of its fins and blink of its eyes.

Hey Jay-o, better check nobody's around. Can't be caught making like a fish.

Jay ran back to the door, checked to make sure the office was still empty, and looked down the corridor toward the kitchen. Bob Lo was definitely not in the house. He closed the metal door to the hatchery and dug out his goggles and snorkel from where he had hidden them behind the fire extinguisher. He returned to the large trough he had chosen, which glowed in a shaft of sunlight, two rainbows in each of its corners.

He slipped off his shoes, pulled off his socks, T-shirt, and denims, stepped over the rim of the trough, and carefully, very carefully, lowered himself into the water. He placed his foot delicately on a bare patch of sand, taking care not to damage any of Bob Lo's plants. Before he sank deeper in the water, he put on his goggles, slipping the snorkel bit into his mouth, and then gently lowered himself to the bottom of the tank. The fish, at first startled by the interloper, soon recognized Jay. They swam through the billowing red tentacles of his hair, caressed his earlobes, brushed his cheeks, nibbled at his nose, and studied the blinking of his eyes.

Jay hummed—a low, gurgling sound, which began in the back of his throat and then resonated in his nose and skull. The water and walls of the tank amplified the sound until, at last, he was at peace.

Once he was submerged in his tank of bubbles, sunlight, fish, rainbows, and monkey leaves, the world outside ceased to exist for Jay. In the water he could hold bubbles in his hand, study the wrinkles on a gourami, feel a fern brush against the small of his back, and listen to the music of the water.

He no longer thought of his father somewhere in Africa, or the creditors repeatedly dunning for payment, or his mother and her boyfriends, or his grandmother who swallowed spoons, or having to write his final examinations, or—this, the most serious of Jay's anxieties—the hollow, fearful, sickening feeling that engulfed him when he thought about the following year, when he would have to become an adult.

There Jay floated, immersed in a trough filled with tropical fish and gulping at life through a plastic pipe. He wondered if ultimately he would defy nature and begin to grow scales, fins, a tail, and a pair of gills, and become the most startling and original of Bob Lo's collection of tropical fish.

JAY NEEDED THE SOLACE of his watery womb because his grandmother had swallowed some more of the family silver. This time it had not been a mere teaspoon but a soup spoon she had swallowed, washing it down with a little honey. In the previous month the old woman had consumed four sugar spoons, two teaspoons, and one butter knife. This had been her first soup spoon, probably because her daughter-in-law had locked away the small silverware. The spoon was quite an achievement. It meant that the soup ladle was no longer impossible. No one knew why she had developed a taste for silverware; the doctor who had removed the cutlery with the aid of a flexible endoscope had suggested that it might be the beginnings of senility. Jay's suspicion was that his grandmother's sudden peculiar appetite for what had been her wedding gift had something to do with her late husband.

After breakfast that morning, Margaret Watson had been reading the newspaper in the living room when she saw the glint of silver in the old woman's mouth. She screamed, but before she could do anything about it the spoon had disappeared. Margaret, who by now had become an expert in these matters, helped her mother-in-law to kneel on the floor and bend over, as she tried in vain to shake out the spoon before it went too far down the old woman's throat.

Jay heard his mother's scream from upstairs, where he had been struggling through a chapter of history for his final examination. He knew immediately what had happened.

Damn! Granny's done it again. How am I going to finish history if I spend all my life at Emergency?

"Jason! Jason, come down here!" Margaret called up to her son in what Jason thought of as her helpless voice.

"I'm coming, I'm coming," he shouted back wearily, shutting the history book.

"But I took her last time," Margaret fretted, wringing her hands while she wondered whether the neighbors had heard her scream.

"You are her daughter-in-law. That's what daughters-in-law do," Jay said, patting his grandmother's back impatiently and helping her up off the floor onto the sofa while Margaret phoned a taxi service.

"Gran, why do you swallow spoons?" Jay asked quietly.

The old lady settled back in her chair, smiled, burped delicately, and continued with her knitting as if nothing had happened.

"Jason, you know Chuck gave me that set of silver cutlery dinner service for our wedding present?" Jay nodded, while he arranged the cushions around his grandmother. "It was such a beautiful gift! Chuck insisted the silver had to be laid out for every meal. Your grandfather was always a very extravagant man, Jason," she said, shaking her head sadly.

"But why eat them, Gran?" Jay said, exasperated.

"I have my reasons. They may not always be obvious to you young people, but I do have my reasons," she said firmly, paying no attention to Margaret, who had returned and was arguing with Jay about filial responsibility.

"You also have some duties in this house, young man. You are also responsible for what happens to Nana. Just because the men in this family have set a bad example doesn't mean that you have to follow it."

"If you told me exactly what bad example the men in this family have set, I might be able to do something about avoiding it."

"Your grandfather and your uncle are obvious enough, and as for your father . . . Well, I don't want to talk about it."

"'You never talk about *it,* but you always talk about *him* as if he was the it!'"

"Leave your father out of this."

"I didn't bring him into it. You did!"

"Jason, I've told you a hundred times, I don't want to talk about your father."

"I know you don't. It's like pulling teeth from a donkey. All I want to know is why he left, and all I get are evasions. And what has Uncle Peter got to do with the whole mess?"

"I just don't want you to be like your father."

"You're always saying that! Well, who am I supposed to be like, then? Must I be like you? Must I be like Gran? Who the hell is my role model if my father's not around?"

"Jason, you are getting loud. You know how that upsets Nana," Margaret had said, patting the old woman on her back. Her eyes had filled with tears, and her voice had become shriller. "All I'm asking for is a little consideration. You live in this house too. You're not a guest, Jason. You're Nana's grandson," she said reproachfully, which immediately made Jay feel guilty and then angry for feeling guilty.

"It would be nice if you played mother once in a while, instead of worrying about your latest date as if you were still in high school."

Ouch! That's below the belt, Jay-o. Enough. Stop now, before it gets too—

"That's a terrible thing to say, Jason!"

The old woman nodded at that point, knitted a couple of stitches, and then emitted a burp, which surprised them both with its ferocity.

"Are you all right, Granny? Do you want some water?"

"How about some milk, Nana?" Margaret asked.

"You two are always fighting with each other. Always

12

fighting. It's such a pity you can't get along. Such a pity," Gran said.

Shamed by her words, they left the room, but once in the kitchen Margaret again turned angrily on Jay.

"How could you mention Brian in front of Nana? You know she gets upset when you talk about him," she said, jerking open the refrigerator door.

"I never mentioned Brian," Jay said, filling a glass with water.

"Jason, you really are impossible nowadays! I don't know what's gotten into you. And another thing, if you would only fix the van, we'd have some sort of transport instead of having to rely on taxis, but ever since your father left, there the van's stood, cluttering up the backyard and—"

"You're bringing him into the conversation again!"

"—rotting. And Brian would love to give you a hand fixing it up, but do you show the slightest bit of interest? Really, Jason, you could at least be polite to him."

Breathe deeply, grit your teeth, bite the bullet. It's so easy to hurt people, and you have the knack for it, Jay-o. Count to ten: one, two, three, four . . .

A sound much like that of the Green Point foghorn came from the living room, forcing mother and son to pay attention once more to the immediate problem of the silver spoon in Nana's stomach.

"We're just going to have to take her to the hospital right away. It was a soup spoon this time, Jason. It could be serious!"

"Ma, they do this all the time at Groote Schuur. People swallow all sorts of dumb things that the doctors have to fish out, and it's not as if this is Gran's first time. The last time we were at the hospital I heard the nurses call her 'Kitchen Drawers.'"

After Nana had quietly gone through the indignity of having the silver spoon removed from her stomach by a rubber fiber-optics contraption, the three had returned to Observatory, and Jay had stormed out of the house seeking the only refuge he knew.

There he sat in a tank of water, tickling the underbelly of Oscar the goldfish, black angels floating through his red hair, bubbles coming from his mouth, and his mind filled with water, rainbows, and sunlight. In his tank of tropical fish his spoon-swallowing grandmother and hard-pressed mother were no longer problems of consequence to him.

As Bob Lo reached his home and opened the gate, he noticed with irritation that it was not locked. Once again his assistant had not replaced the key on its ledge.

"I've told that kid hundreds of times, 'Put the key back before you go into the house and lock the gate.' And does he listen? Does he pay attention? No! He carries on as if everyone in the world was his friend," Bob Lo grumbled, locking the gate behind him and entering the house.

Oblivious of the disarray, he, too, walked straight down the passage toward the hatchery. In his office he paused. He looked around for a chair and, placing it quietly against the metal door, climbed onto it and peered through the small window above the door.

"Just as I thought. He's blowing bloody bubbles again. These kids can never make up their minds. They don't know if they want to be fish, fowl, or good red herring."

Muttering to himself, he dragged the chair noisily back to the desk, rattled some test tubes, opened and closed the office door several times, and then slammed it. Finally, he sat down in his chair and waited for his assistant to appear.

Wondering as usual why his boss always made such a noise when he came into the office, Jay scrambled out of the tank to find the towel he kept hidden in the hatchery. He dried himself, dressed quickly, and then hurriedly smoothed away any traces of his presence in the tank and hid his goggles and snorkel. On his way to the office he assumed a casual air, which he hoped would convince Bob Lo that everything was as it should be.

He opened the metal door and, on seeing Bob Lo, stopped as if surprised.

"Oh, there you are," Jay said nonchalantly. "Did you get the feed from the dam?"

"No. I wasn't at the dam, and I thought you had to study for your big exams and wouldn't be coming in today."

Bob Lo looked carefully at his assistant. Jay avoided meeting his employer's eyes by hunting around his desk as if looking for something.

"Oh? History's old hat. I'm not that worried. Math is going to be tough, but that's in ten days' time."

"Just don't be so Harry-casual now, and then find out it's too late when you don't know the answers." Bob Lo angrily shuffled some papers on his desk and swore under his breath. Jay suddenly remembered the only thing that could make his boss this angry.

"You were at one of your breeder's meetings—"

"Nincompoops! Bloody monkeys who think they know everything about tropical fish! One of them even thought he could tell me I was wasting my time and being too fin-icky. Blooming monkey! He wouldn't be able to spot a black angel if it nibbled at his nose!"

He's off again. Keep a straight face, Jay-o. Get me back into the light, music, and water. Clumsy, everything feels so clumsy. Words heavy, movement stiff, thoughts like gum boots in mud. Come back, rainbow water and my Princess Moonlight Gou-rami. King Knoi, we have not finished our watery discussion about my marriage to your daughter . . .

"Bloody donkeys, the lot of them! They think they can sell tropical fish like tins of sardines. No integrity!"

He rattled and clacked away, just as the wooden mobile that hung from the office ceiling did when wind passed through its beads. When he was angry, his hands would copy the flying pattern of two butterflies, as the wrinkles around his mouth and eyes contracted and expanded.

"Quacks, the whole blooming lot of them!" As Jay turned to reenter the hatchery he added, "You've got water behind your ears, Jay. You're dripping."

"It's hot in there, Bob. I just splashed some water on my face."

"Uh-huh, and that monkey fern hanging from your ear?"

Jay quickly raised his hand to his ear, realizing too late that this was his employer's idea of a joke. Bob Lo chuckled as Jay blushed and turned to go back into the hatchery.

"Have you fed the neons yet?"

"No, I was busy cleaning out the black angels. The water's pretty dirty."

"I've noticed the river water we get from Du Toit's Kloof is finished. We must make another journey soon, but now it's time for work. Oh, and if you leave the gate unlocked one more time I will dock your pay and take the key away for a month, okay?"

"Okay. Sorry."

"You had better be, you monkey. Come on, we've serious work to do, and I also want you to do something special today."

They cleaned the troughs, refilled them with water, moved fish from tank to tank, dipped nets into live bait, and fed the fish. Once Bob Lo had calmed down, the two worked together with hardly a word between them. Often on these occasions Bob Lo would tire of the chores and retreat to his office, close the door, turn on the infrared light, and study the journey of the male sperm of the spotted tiger as it fertilized the female eggs. His office would

16

glow with the red light, while he worked on his secrets of procreation and cross-fertilization, and Jay would have the hatchery to himself.

Someone else might have done this mundane job perfunctorily and been bored. Not Jay. Because he was possessed of an unusual talent for invention, there he was, diligently pouring clean water into a tank, planting the monkey fern, smoothing out the sand, plucking water snails from the plants, and . . .

Oscar, go away! You shall not eat the royal lettuce while King Khoi's back is turned. Nor shall you take over the Khoi kingdom and nibble it barren. And so the great Hand of Man swept clean the waters of Khoi kingdom, protecting the people from mishap. But a sacrifice was demanded. The beautiful Princess Moonlight Gourami had to be transported to another world. That was the prize all fishes of Khoi had to pay for clean water. No longer would she glide among her subjects; no longer would they gaze upon her loveliness. The Hand of Man would take her from them.

With a deft flick of his hand Jay swept up a tiny gourami and dropped it into the adjoining fish tank.

Deep into the murky waters the poor princess was thrown. Strangers swam up to her, butting the royal nose, unaware of her royal lineage. Alone she swam, disoriented and fearful for her life. Deep in the crevices of the tank lurked the dark shape of the Mighty Eel moving in the depths of her new world. She knew of his evil, and with a shiver of her beautiful tail she fled, nosing the roof of the world, searching for the way back to her own. But she was trapped. The Hand of Man had decreed.

Jay had a wonderfully fishy imagination. No Saturday would go by without his adding further elaborations to the world of King Khoi, Oscar, and Princess Moonlight. Bob Lo would often look up from his work to watch Jay, his head bent over a tank and his hands moving slowly

17

through the water, and wonder what it was that his assistant found so fascinating.

Jay was capable of creating a fishy fiction that would last all morning and afternoon. Often at the end of the day Bob Lo would have to remind him that it was six o'clock, time to go home.

Although Jay never fully understood his employer's intense love for his fish, he was always impressed by Bob Lo's enthusiasm when a new batch of neon tetras was born or when a successful strain of black angel was developed. He knew that for himself the hatchery was a hideaway, not a passion. It was his watery womb, where he waited for life to begin. He had no passion. Yes, he enjoyed the work, but he did it because there was nothing else to do.

In the Topical Fish Emporium he avoided the flying debris convulsing his country. South Africa was shedding its old ways, and to many it was a bewildering place. What had once been clearly defined was now all confusion. The markings of fish no longer determined which tank they should live in. King Khoi was negotiating with a multitude of black angels. Politicians were apologizing through the national news media, church leaders were praying for forgiveness for past transgressions. The government had unbanned the enemy and turned him into a negotiator.

Change was everywhere. Cape Town had the feel of a city preparing for either a carnival or a bloodbath. How did you alter your point of view overnight? How did you readdress issues that were once as clear as day and which suddenly had become as murky as mud? For Jay it was easy: Head for the water, light, and rainbows.

"I want you to go see someone today," Bob Lo said, looking up from his microscope as Jay entered the office.

"Oh yes?"

"Your uncle, in fact. Peter Hodges."

Taken aback, Jay stared at Bob Lo.

"What?"

"You heard me. Your uncle, Peter Hodges."

"You mean my half uncle, Uncle Peter the Pumpkin Eater?" Jay was dumbfounded at the casual way Bob Lo had brought up the explosive issue of his father's half brother.

"I don't believe in half family members. You are or you are not blood. There are no halves," Bob Lo said, returning to his microscope to scrutinize the wriggling of King Khoi's sperm.

"Well, he's only the uncle everybody in my family loves to hate. Not that I know why. All I know is we're not well off and we used to be. We've creditors knocking all day at our door demanding payment, and that's got something to do with the Pumpkin Eater who changed his family name. Mom would have a fit if she knew I went to see him, and Gran would probably start on the knives and forks if she heard about it."

Jay could not contain himself. He babbled on while Bob Lo waited patiently.

"You finished?"

"Yup!" Jay said without looking up.

Bob Lo glanced over at his assistant and raised his eyebrows. He picked up one of the knitting needles he kept in a jar and pursued some of the sperm wriggling around in the glass dish under his microscope. Delicately he lifted a million sperm on the needle's point and placed them in a small tank at his elbow.

"It's about that box," Bob Lo said. "I want you to visit your uncle in Camps Bay and ask him for a box."

"A box?"

"Well, actually, it's made out of yellowwood. It's larger than a shoe box but smaller than a trunk," he said, as if he were repeating someone else's words. "Peter Hodges will know what you're talking about. As eldest son he must have been responsible for your grandfather's possessions after he died."

Bob Lo swirled the knitting needle around in the tank of water and then, with a small net, lifted several female neon tetras out of another tank.

A Coke bottle smashing against a wall. Was it the bottle exploding, or was it a gunshot? A father's angry face. A mother's tears. The back of Uncle Peter's bald head. A little boy on his bed staring at the ceiling, fighting back the tears, shaken by what he had done.

"You mustn't say who sent you. You have merely come for what rightfully belongs to you. It's your inheritance."

Bob Lo gently let the net of female neon tetras down into the tank where the invisible million sperm were frantically searching for them and gazed into the fish tank as the fertilization of the females presumably took place.

"What's in this yellowwood box?"

"How should I know? It belongs to you. Your grandfather left it to you."

"Gramps? He left me something?"

"If Peter Hodges asks you how you know about it—and he will—say you read about it in a letter from your grandfather. This is something you must do on your own. You understand?"

Gramps left me something? Those last days stroking his wrinkled hand, bending forward to feel the movement of his lips against my cheek as he tried to speak. I couldn't understand his muttering, and the smell of his illness made it hard to stay for very long. Chuck left me something.

"Jay, what's the matter with you? Don't you understand?"

"Not really."

"Man, it's bloody simple. You take a bus to Camps Bay, look up your uncle, and say hello. You haven't seen him in ten years, but he'll recognize you. Then you ask him for the yellowwood box. Say that your grandfather promised it to you, and that's that. It's simple."

"But Gramps died six months ago. Why didn't you tell me then?"

Bob Lo slapped the knitting needle down, dried his hands on his trousers, and looked at Jay impatiently.

"It wasn't the right time."

"But I don't even know where he lives. He's hardly on my mother's Christmas card list."

"Here's a phone book. Don't be so useless. Look it up: P. Hodges, Camps Bay. There can't be that many."

"This is incredible! Mom would have a fit and Gran would blow a gasket if they knew I was actually going to see the Pumpkin Eater."

"I want you to go today. I'll give you the rest of the afternoon off," Bob Lo said as he stood up and went to the hatchery door.

"Today! But—"

"You have to go today. Your uncle may not be around another time. He travels a lot."

"Couldn't I just phone him and ask him to send it by mail?"

"No! You will have to go to see him and pick it up personally."

"Gramps told you that?"

"Yes. Now go. I'll see you next week."

Bob Lo disappeared into the hatchery.

Jay flicked through the phone book and ran his fingers down the H's. He found the address he was looking for. He wrote it down on a piece of paper, put on his denim jacket, and left the Emporium.

Peter, Peter, Pumpkin Eater, had a wife and couldn't keep her . . .

On his way back through Darien Square, Jay stopped opposite Jenny Bam's cottage. Hanging onto his courage with both hands, he once again went up to the gate. He wondered whether he would be able to put together a coherent sentence should she appear.

Steady, Jay-o, the world is not going to crumble and spin off its axis if she comes out and talks to you. Feel those hormones having a party! Nothing like behaving like a lovesick idiot to get the old heart pumping up a storm.

"She's still not here."

Oh no, it's the boy wonder who's named after a pair of jeans!

"Go away, brat. No one's talking to you."

"I watched you come across the square. I knew you were going to stop. When are you going to take me to the cemetery?"

"Tomorrow. I'm busy today."

"It's never tomorrow."

"I promise. Now shut up. You're too young to be so cheeky."

"I'm nine and a half. That's old enough for anything."

"Is that right?" Jay looked at Levi's face and thought again how unlike this boy was from any other nine-year-old he'd met.

"Is that a real promise, or a lying promise?" Levi insisted.

Ouch! This boy knows where to find the soft spot. Always straight to the heart.

Levi regarded Jay steadily. It felt as if he were scrutinizing Jay's innermost thoughts. Levi had no friends his own age but preferred the company of older people who were also outsiders. Jay knew that he had been classified in this category and resented Levi for recognizing his own personal inadequacy. The cheerless boy perpetually sought him out, and Jay could not shed the guilt he always felt when he did not respond to Levi's attempts at friendship.

"It's a real one. I promise. I'll pick you up early tomorrow morning. You'd better tell your mother."

"She won't mind. She probably won't be here."

Behind Levi the front door of the Bam cottage opened and a man stepped out. He called something back into the house and strode toward the gate.

Oh no, it's the good-looking boyfriend. I hate confident, handsome men who drive high-powered cars!

Gary Martin walked buoyantly down the front path with a self-satisfied smile on his tanned face. He wore a tank top and a pair of denim shorts that showed off his muscular torso and brown legs. He had a salon-designed mop of sun-blond hair, cropped around the back of the neck and ears but left thick on top. His magazine good looks were spoiled only by his closely set blue eyes.

"Hi, kids," he said as Jay stepped aside to let him through the gate.

"Jay's not a kid," Levi said, glaring malevolently at his mother's boyfriend.

"Hey, I'm so sorry, Denim," Gary said with mock courtesy. "Bye, kid and teenager."

He opened the door of the black V-8 four-wheel truck that was parked outside the cottage and pulled away from the curb with a screech of tires.

"What a jerk!" Jay said, watching the truck shoot the stop sign and disappear around the corner. "He'll kill somebody driving like that."

"And my mother wants to marry him," Levi said disparagingly. Then, reverting to his main interest of the moment, he looked at Jay. "You're not going to forget about tomorrow. You promise?"

"I promise, Lee. Early tomorrow morning."

The boy nodded, turned, and went into the house.

Oh sorrowful day, without the joy of Jenny Bam's belly button in one of her summer creations! But on to other interesting missions, Jay-o! Onward, onward, over the neck, to the land of milk, honey, white beaches, and credit cards.

On the way to see Peter Hodges in Camps Bay Jay lost his right flip-flop. He was trying to get off the city bus, which had stopped on Camps Bay Drive, but in front of him, blocking the way, was an old Greek woman dressed in black. In one hand she carried a walking stick and in the other a string bag filled with shopping. She waddled slowly down the aisle, unperturbed by the bus driver's irritated gaze or Jay's efforts to pass her.

"Hurry up, granny," the bus driver said as she drew near the door.

The old woman ignored him but appealed to Jay.

"You help an old woman?" she asked, handing Jay her string bag.

"Yes, of course."

Her bony hand fastened tightly onto Jay's wrist. Her fingers felt surprisingly cool.

"Such a strong young man," she said as Jay helped her down the steps. "Such a strong young man. You must have many girlfriends, hey?" Her face was close to Jay's. "You're the one," she suddenly whispered.

"Will you and your granny please hurry up," the bus driver urged impatiently. With Jay half on the step, half on the road, the old woman jerked suddenly at his wrist. His foot caught on the step, and he lost his balance and his flip-flop. As the bus pulled away he could see his sandal lying on the step. He shouted and tried to chase

24

the bus, but the old woman's grip on his wrist held him back.

"You're the one," she repeated. "I saw red hair. You're the one."

Before Jay could think of anything to say she let go of his wrist, tapped him smartly on the shoulder, snatched the string bag out of his hand, and walked off down the street.

"Crazy," Jay muttered, watching her turn a corner and rubbing his wrist, which ached from the strength of her grip.

So there he stood on Camps Bay Drive looking for number 118, wearing only one flip-flop. He briefly considered going back home, but this idea didn't appeal to him. His curiosity had been aroused by Bob Lo's remarks, and he was too eager to see what his grandfather had left him to worry about a lost flip-flop. Anyway, he didn't plan to spend long with his uncle. He tried smoothing down his hair, but as usual it refused to be tidied.

Camps Bay Drive wound up the slope of the mountain, and all along the road immense houses—large, two-storied, privileged living spaces of the rich—jockeyed for the best view of the Atlantic Ocean.

Only illustrious folk
could live without a moat,
in a high-walled palace,
with a swimming pool,
two motor cars, and a boat!

These were not old cottages done up by yuppies in the Observatory fashion. These were the homes of the rich, who spent money nonchalantly on landscape gardeners, security systems, cordless telephones, and Afghan hounds. Crossing the cradle between Table Mountain and Signal Hill brought one into a world quite distinct from the bustle of Cape Town and the teeming townships east of the city. The crowded, often run-down cottages of Jay's suburb were replaced here by space, glossy newness, and the clean breath of sea breezes.

Jay hobbled along Camps Bay Drive knowing he didn't belong in this neighborhood.

I am not here walking up the road in Camps Bay. I am not looking for Peter Pumpkin Eater, the Unmentionable in the Watson house. I am not about to collect a yellowwood box left to me by Gramps. This is not you, Jay-o. It's an impostor who has taken over your body, lost your flip-flop, and gone on a walkabout to Camps Bay. You, Jay-o, take a back seat.

Finding Peter Hodges's house, a two-story building half-way up Camps Bay Drive, was easier than Jay had expected. A large brass *118* glinted on the white wall surrounding the property.

Jay paused before he opened the gate at the bottom of a long flight of steps and looked at his uncle's mansion. The house screamed money. Caught in double French doors opening onto a balcony was the reflection of a swimming pool surrounded by white tiles. Spreading out beyond the pool was a meticulously tended garden, lush with an over-whelming display of roses.

Without a sandal Jay felt naked, scruffy, and poor. He hoped that his uncle wasn't at home. Slowly he climbed the steps, very much aware of the house looming over him. Halfway up the steps, he stopped to admire the white beach and palm trees of Camps Bay and the waves of the Atlantic crashing down on the shore.

The front door was oak, and on it was a large brass knocker in the shape of a fist. He lifted the knocker and then hesitated. A surge of panic rushed through him. He wanted to replace the brass fist gently, run back down the steps, and catch a bus to Observatory.

Don't knock. Turn around and go back where you belong.

You're not welcome, Jay-o. You come from the wrong side of the family, the wrong side of town. Leave . . .

The brass knocker slipped out of his hand and banged so loudly on the door that Jay jumped. He stared at the knocker, which felt as if it had been pulled from his hand. Once committed, he knocked again, this time enjoying the deep reverberations his action produced inside the house.

He waited, looking down at his bare foot and wondering if his half uncle would recognize him after ten years.

Snot-nosed seven-year-old that I was. You bought me a science set, with miniature test tubes, crystal-making chemicals, and a small Bunsen burner. My mother disapproved; I was clumsy. You showed me how to put iodine crystals in water and how to get purple fingers. You laughed when I singed my eyebrows.

The door was opened by a young black woman in a white uniform. Behind her the white tiles surrounding the swimming pool continued into the interior. A glass chandelier hung from the ceiling, and under a large watercolor of a misty beach scene a glass-topped aluminum table supported a vase of white hibiscus. An aluminum chair stood beside the table. The walls were airbrushed a creamy shade of white. A sense of luxurious coolness bounced off the floors and walls of Peter Hodges's entrance hall, and the woman's black face shone out against the surrounding whiteness.

"Can I help you?"

"Hi. Yes, you can. I've come to see Peter Hodges. This is where he lives?"

"Yes."

"My name is Jay Watson. I'm his nephew."

The woman, startled, looked more carefully at Jay, and then her eyes traveled down to his feet. She hesitated for a moment before she opened the door wider.

27

"Won't you please come in, Mr. Watson. I'll tell Mr. Hodges that you're here. Please wait over there." She indicated the aluminum chair.

Jay moved into the entrance hall and sat down as he had been told. He watched the young woman go up a flight of stairs to the second story. On the wall across from him another large canvas swirled with bright colors. The house was quiet once the woman had closed the front door; Jay could hear the ticking of a clock. He hated just sitting and waiting, so he got up and went over to a doorway opening out from the entrance hall.

Through the door Jay could see a sitting room with leather couches, more modern artwork on the walls, and another glass-topped coffee table. On it was a pack of Tarot cards laid out in a circle, in the center of which a single card had been placed. Something moving in one of the corners of the room caught Jay's attention. A large crystal was slowly rotating on a pedestal. Caught in a beam of light directed onto it, it reflected multicolored flashes that crept along the walls.

Ladies and gentlemen, laid on for display: the art gallery of Peter the Pumpkin Eater. Not only a lover of paintings, the Pumpkin Eater is also—surprise, surprise!—a lover of rainbows.

At the far end of the room was a large, rectangular aquarium glowing with blue light. The tank's flickering fluorescence enticed Jay and, forgetting he was a stranger in the house, he crossed the room to look into the luminous blue water.

Jay found he was looking, with growing disgust, at a tank full of tropical fish hybrids. Trained by Bob Lo to appreciate the beauty of tropical fish, he noted, horrified, goldfish with enlarged foreheads, a school of guppies with truncated bodies and inflated genitals, and a fish with a featherlike dorsal fin at the side of its bulbous body. In one corner there was a two-headed goldfish, in another corner a King Khoi with enormous, sorrowful eyes bulging out of its skull. A fish floated by with an elongated nose, and he instantly recognized it as a cross between a snout-nosed elephant and a guppy. One small fish had an enormous frayed tail that dwarfed its tiny torso, and a flash of pure white signaled an albino goldfish that was ghostlike and transparent.

To Jay, Peter Hodges's tropical fish were the mutants, which Bob Lo so despised. They had been developed to accentuate some genetic defect. Every fish was deformed in some way. The aquarium was a tropical-fish horror show.

"So you are also a lover of tropical fish, Jason?"

The voice came from behind Jay, who looked back, startled, to see Peter Hodges standing and watching him from the doorway of the sitting room.

"Sorry. I saw the tank, and I had to see what was in it. I hope you don't mind."

"Make yourself at home," the older man said wryly.

Peter Hodges crossed the room. He grinned as he shook hands with Jay.

"How are you? Your carrottop hasn't changed at all, I see."

He was a tall, muscular man, dressed in cream clothes, which displayed his tan. Jay immediately identified him as a denizen of Camps Bay by the gold chain around his neck.

As Peter Hodges bent over the aquarium Jay noticed the rows of hair follicles that had been carefully sewn into his scalp.

"So what do you think of my collection of exquisite little monsters?"

"Interesting."

"Ah, you're still the polite Watson child, Jason. Is that all my fish are? 'Interesting.' How humiliating! And after all my trouble. Don't they arouse anything stronger than mere

29

interest in you? Can't you see the potential for genetic engineering in crossbreeding? The imagination is set free to produce something magnificently ugly, such as our two-headed little fellow here, or to defy nature's sense of balance and achieve something uniquely beautiful, like our large-tailed gourami there. With the power of mutation in your own hands, the possibilities are endless. It is surely more than just interesting, don't you think?"

"I think it's gross and unnatural."

" 'Unnatural,' " Peter Hodges said meditatively, as if Jay had uttered a new word. "So, because something doesn't agree with your view of what is right and proper, you declare, with a certain self-righteousness, that it is unnatural. How bigoted of you, Jason. A regular little fascist. You're just like your father. By the way, how is Jack?"

Peter Hodges moved away from the aquarium to sit down on the couch behind the coffee table. He stretched his arms out along the back of the couch, crossed his legs, and benevolently regarded his nephew. He was supremely confident, a king in his palace, a master of men.

"I haven't heard from my father. He doesn't write often," Jay said, stung by his uncle's question.

"Oh yes, of course. He's exploring Africa, isn't he?"

"Yes."

"And he's not traveling alone, I understand?" Peter Hodges said, quizzically.

You laughed when I singed my eyebrows, and you're laughing at me now. My mother crying as she swept up the broken glass and wiped the wall. You were going bald in those days, Pumpkin Eater.

"No, he's not. He's hooked up with a university student who fancied the idea of traveling through Africa with an older man on a motorbike—as you well know," Jay replied angrily.

"That's better, Jason, much better. I thought maybe you

were incapable of emotion. It's good to see that you have developed some of the Watson fire to match your hair. Come, sit down. Why, I think it must be almost ten years since I've heard from your family. We used to be quite close, you know. No, of course you wouldn't remember. Let me see, you must have been about six when I last saw you."

"Seven."

"So you're seventeen. A good age to be. Stay away from the twenties. They're wicked. Come, sit down. We have a lot to talk about."

Oh no we don't, Uncle. I want to take what is mine and get out of this bizarre house and away from this bizarre man.

Jay sat down awkwardly on the edge of the seat opposite his uncle.

"I must say I'm surprised to have a visitor from . . ." Peter Hodges stopped speaking, uncrossed his legs, and leaned forward. Jay thought he saw panic flash across his uncle's face, but the idea of rich Peter Hodges feeling threatened by a young nephew was so ludicrous that Jay assumed he'd been mistaken.

"Where is your sandal?"

Jay looked defensively down at his bare foot, naked and dirty against the costly Persian carpet. He felt foolish; he wished he had not climbed the steps to this mansion but instead had caught the bus back to Observatory. He was too busy trying to hide his own embarrassment to suspect that a change had taken place in his uncle.

Peter Hodges stood up and went to stand behind the couch. He was no longer relaxed, patronizing, and elegant, but tense and on his guard.

"I lost it on the way here. I was helping an old woman off a bus, and I lost it. I'm sorry; it looks dreadful, but I didn't really intend to stay long."

"Why did you come here?"

Jay looked more closely at his uncle, who seemed to have paled slightly. He wondered what had happened to change his uncle's tone of mocking geniality.

"I read a letter from my grandfather; it said you had a box for me. It's made out of yellowwood. Gramps said that you would know what I meant."

Peter Hodges relaxed slightly and walked over to a liquor cabinet.

"I must apologize. I've been extremely rude. Would you like something to drink? A beer, perhaps?" he asked, turning to Jay, who was confused by his uncle's second sudden change of tone.

"I'd like a Coke, please."

Peter Hodges rang a silver bell, and the young black woman appeared in the doorway. He asked her to bring the Coke and some ice, poured himself a drink, and then walked back to the center of the room with his drink in his hand.

"Can I ask you something personal, Jason? Are you superstitious?"

The question took Jay by surprise. He looked down at the circle of Tarot cards on the coffee table. Their symbols were meaningless to him.

What trap are you laying for me now, Uncle?

"If you mean do I believe in fortune-telling, no, I'm not."

"I'm not talking about fortune-telling, Jason, but about creating your own reality."

Peter Hodges placed his drink on the table and turned the card lying in the center of the ring of cards to face toward Jay. "You see, I knew you were coming. I was told you would, one day. In a way I've been expecting you. What do you think of that?"

Puzzled, and feeling himself being drawn into alien

territory, Jay glanced down at the card his uncle had turned around.

"Look closely at the boy on the card, Jason. What do you see?"

"A boy holding sticks in one hand and some kind of golden skin in the other."

"Is that all?"

"Yes."

"Are you sure that's all?"

"Yes!"

"Look at the boy's feet."

Jay focused on the feet of the boy on the card. He was wearing only one sandal. Jay looked up and shrugged.

"So?"

"It's a hero from one of the Greek legends, Jason and the Golden Fleece." Peter Hodges paused, waiting for Jay to respond. When he didn't, Hodges picked up the cards on the table, shuffled them, fanned them in his hand, and held them out to Jay.

"Now choose a card."

Jay stood up and backed away from the table.

"Oh, come now! Don't be afraid simply because you don't understand."

Made to feel trapped and foolish by his uncle's disdain, Jay sat down again, leaned forward, pulled a card from the pack, and flipped it over onto the table.

The card Jay had selected depicted a female figure with three faces, crowned by a diadem of the moon in its three phases. Her hair was silver, and she was clothed in white robes, which fell into a pool at her feet. Beside her stood a three-headed dog; a crab was crawling out of the pool. The sky behind her was dark, lit only by the luminescence of her crown.

"Just as I thought!" Peter Hodges exulted. "You've drawn the moon card! It represents the element of feeling and is

a symbol of the mysterious watery depths of the unconscious. You must surrender to the power of the moon and
be content to walk in the dark without light. You are in
contact with the ancient goddess of the underworld, Hecate, ruler of the moon, magic, and enchantment."

As Peter Hodges intoned the words, Jay felt himself
being subjected to an almost mystic power.

"The card of the moon is the card of gestations, suggest-
ing confusion, anxiety, bewilderment, and auguring a time
of uncertainties. You are in the thrall of the unconscious
and are helpless. Wait! Cling to the elusive images of
dreams. Hope and believe."

Jay stared at the card Peter had placed in front of him.

*That's exactly what I've been feeling—confused, like I'm wait-
ing for something. Come on, Jay-o, where's that old skepticism
of yours? It feels right, though, as if someone is trying to get
through to me. Don't let him get you offtrack, Jay-o. You came
for the box, remember.*

"This is very interesting, but all I came for was the box,"
said Jay, throwing off his uncle's influence and pushing the
card away from him.

Peter Hodges took the card off the table and returned it
to the pack. He leaned back on the couch and studied Jay
carefully.

"What do you know about Chuck Watson's precious
box?"

"Nothing, only that he wanted me to have it. I don't
understand why he didn't give it to me when he was alive."

The young woman came back with a tray that held a
glass of Coke and a bowl of ice. She placed the tray on the
table and left. Jay picked up the glass, dropped a few
pieces of ice into the Coke, and put the glass back on the
table.

He had become aware of the changed atmosphere in the
room, and of how carefully his uncle was watching him.

Peter Hodges was no longer merely tolerating him, and Jay no longer felt so inadequate. The implications of his uncle's changed attitude gave him confidence. He knew without a doubt that something had badly disturbed Peter Hodges. He was determined to press home the slight advantage he seemed to have gained over his uncle.

"What do you know about me, Jason? What have your father and mother told you about Peter Hodges, your half uncle?"

"Not a lot. You and my father ran Grandfather's business for a while after he disappeared. The business went sour, and my father lost a lot of money. You obviously didn't," Jay replied, glancing around the room.

There's something else crawling out of the bottom of my mind. I grope, I strain forward, look over the edge of the abyss, down into the swirling chasm. Something lies at the bottom.

"This"—Peter Hodges gestured around the room— "happened fairly recently, and has no connection with that old story."

I don't believe you, Uncle. I don't know why, but you're lying. Why is that bead of perspiration rolling through the rows of your artificial hair in a room as cool as this one? You're not afraid of me, are you?

"I've come for the box Grandfather left me," Jay repeated firmly.

"Ah, the yellowwood box your grandfather valued so highly. Well, I'm sorry to disappoint you, Jason, but I haven't got it."

"You haven't got it?"

"No, I never had it. In fact, I've never laid eyes on this mythical box," Peter Hodges said dismissively. "I tried to buy it when the old man's stuff was auctioned off, but I was unlucky, and someone else got it. The old fool didn't have a lot to leave, as you know. He had led a singularly

35

useless life. I thought it very noble of Margaret to take him in after he had his stroke, but then your mother was always a very generous woman."

Why do you speak of Gramps as a fool? He was your father. Or do you choose to disown your own father, just as I am trying to disown mine?

"Well, I'm sorry that I've wasted your time." Jay stood up to go.

"Wait, you can't go yet. You haven't had any of your Coke and, besides, this conversation is just beginning to get interesting."

"I really should be going."

Jay was determined to get out of the house. He knew that he looked ridiculous, with only one sandal and his hair sticking out all over the place. However, he also knew that in some way he had unsettled his uncle. The questions Peter Hodges had asked had been too searching for the mere purpose of reestablishing acquaintance with a long-lost member of the family. No, there was a new edge to Peter Hodges's voice and a tension in his manner, as if he had gone on the defensive. Jay moved purposefully toward the door, trying to ignore the social handicap of his single flip-flop.

"What if I could tell you where your grandfather's yellowwood box was?" came his uncle's voice from behind him.

Jay stopped and turned around. "You like to play games, Uncle. Why don't you simply tell me all you know, and I'll leave and get out of your life."

"Oh no, I think it's too late for that, Nephew. You're back in my life and I in yours. We have a common destiny; we are bound by the blood we share. I have changed my name, lived in another country, but there's no escaping blood ties. Our bloodline is inextricably tied up with our fate. When I said earlier that I'd been expecting you, I was not playing games. I meant what I said. You see, Jason, I know why you are here: You've come to challenge me."

Jay's feelings changed from irritation to bewilderment. He knew he was not equipped to play his uncle's semantic snakes and ladders. Displaced from his own familiar world into the alien territory of his uncle's house, the neon aquarium, and the moon card, Jay felt hopelessly lost. But he sensed something of deep significance in his uncle's words.

"From that look on your face I can see you haven't the faintest idea of what I'm talking about."

"Look, I was told to come here and fetch something that belonged to me. That's all I know. I didn't come here to be psychoanalyzed, or be shown some stupid card, or even to have a drink with you. I came to fetch a box my grandfather left me. It's as simple as that."

Peter Hodges smiled. Then he threw his head back and laughed out loud at Jay, who stared at him blankly.

"Oh, come now, Jason! Don't be so bloody naïve. You know as well as I do why you're here. You are bursting with questions. You want to know all the gory details, every rotten moment, all the whys and hows, and then you want to crucify me."

"I do not!" shouted Jay. "I don't know what you are talking about. I don't want to know anything about *it*, either, whatever *it* is. I came here because my dead grandfather wanted me to pick up something. That's all!"

More confused than ever, Jay headed for the entrance hall. He had to get out of this house. Images were flooding back too rapidly.

The back of a naked woman sitting on a chair with a funny hat on her head. The boy is thirsty. He wants something out of the fridge. The fridge is locked. I spy with my little eye.

"You really don't know? Well, well, that is a surprise."

Peter Hodges no longer sounded so aggressive. Without

37

turning his head, Jay knew his uncle had followed him into the entrance hall. Jay reached for the doorknob.

The naked woman starts to turn on the chair. Her head is cocked back, the hat is slipping off, she is turning around, slowly. The boy's thirst disappears. He needs to know. The back of the naked woman rivets him. He cannot move. He has to see her face.

"I have misjudged your parents, Jason. Forgive me."

The new tone in his uncle's voice stopped Jay once more. He did not turn around, but stood looking into the reverse side of the spy hole in the front door.

"Your grandfather's belongings were auctioned at Miller's Auction, in Adderley Street. He wanted it that way. Your father was supposed to get the yellowwood box, but he had lost himself in Africa by then. Somehow the box got thrown in with the rest of the stuff. I have the address of the man who bought a lot of it. I didn't do anything about it because I didn't think the old man's things were that important to anyone."

Jay turned around to speak, but the room was empty. His uncle had gone back into the house somewhere.

Go, leave, get out. Fly down the steps, back to Observatory, Jay-o. Take a dive into the nearest tank. Go!

Jay could not leave without that address. He had to stick it out a little longer, just a little longer, like Peter Hodges's fishes, those horrible imperfections, gliding through their own nightmare.

A loud splash, almost as if someone had dropped a stone into water, came from Peter Hodges's fish tank. Jay stopped and turned around to see what fishy agitation had made the noise. He walked across the hall to the sitting room and looked at the aquarium across the room. He noticed water on the floor around it. It seemed to be glowing more brightly. From where he stood he could see only blurred floating shapes.

Radioactive topical fish:
blast them with a bit of nuclear waste,
and see what new nightmare shapes mutate.

"Here's the address I got at the auction," said Peter Hodges from behind Jay. "They're not allowed to give out the names of buyers, so I had to pay plenty to get hold of this. Go and find the yellowwood box, and when you've found it come and talk to me again. I'm sure we'll have a lot more to say to each other next time."

Peter Hodges handed a card to Jay. Without looking at it and without another word Jay hobbled past his uncle and out the front door. As the door shut behind him he kicked off his flip-flop. Barefoot, he hurtled down the steps two at a time.

The sun was low over the Atlantic, and a path of fire stretching from the horizon to the white sand glinted on the water. On the beach people were walking their dogs, throwing Frisbees, or packing up their picnic baskets. Out at sea a few boys in wet suits were catching their last wave of the day.

Jay paid no attention. He was running down the road as fast as he could. Without looking at it still, he stuffed the card into the pocket of his jeans. The first thing he became aware of was the pavement burning his bare feet.

Water. To the water, Jay-o. Get into the great ocean of water, make like a fish, swim away. Too many thoughts at once.

He jumped onto the white sand and ran toward the waterline. As he ran he stripped off his clothes. In his underpants he hit the water, running, and dived into a wave as it crashed onto the shallow surf. The water was cold—Atlantic ice. His breath caught in his throat, and he came up for air before diving deeper. Underwater, he opened his eyes. He could see nothing, only turbulence, fierce churning, as wave after wave broke above him. He surfaced again, choking on salt water, and with grit in his eyes. He had been seeking rainbows, cool gurgling, and the Princess Moonlight Gourami. All he had found was turmoil.

Gasping for breath he turned back to the shore. The waves pummeled him, forcing him beneath the surface again. He struck out for the beach and, as soon as he could feel the ground beneath his feet, waded out of the water.

Panting and exhausted, with the taste of salt in his mouth, he remembered the moon card.

I have entered the oceanic realm where confusion reigns. I am not like the crab and the three-headed dog. I cannot survive there.

He was beginning to shiver. The sun's last rays were no longer warm, and the dusk air was cool. He dried himself with his shirt and made for the warm rocks to watch the setting sun. The golden circle slowly sank into the sea, leaving behind it traces of amber and pink in the clouds on the horizon.

Only after he had rested for some time did Jay take out the card Peter Hodges had given him. He read the address: Arthur Jacobs, Zone 13, number 39. Lingelethu, Khayelitsha.

He lives in a township!

This was a surprise to Jay. He had assumed that whoever had bought his grandfather's belongings would be white. An image of shacks lining the N2 highway out to Somerset West came into his mind. Then other, more disturbing, images of burned-out taxis, dead people on the sidewalk, burning shanties, policemen retreating from an angry mob. He had never been to Khayelitsha. All he knew was what he read in the newspaper and saw on television and had conveniently pushed out of his mind. White boys had no reason to go into the townships.

How the hell am I going to get into Khayelitsha, let alone find Zone 13, number 39? And what's this, Jay-o? A little scared, too, at the thought of going into the township?

Jay looked back toward the mountain, at the houses crowded in the shadow of the twelve apostle peaks. He was looking for Peter Hodges's mansion and, as if to help him, the sinking sun caught the French windows of his uncle's white house. The sun slowly set and left Camps Bay flickering in a dusky afterglow.

Blood ties. Since you are partly my blood, Uncle, I want to know why our family has shut you out. And as for the yellow-wood box, I will find the gift from my grandfather. I will track it down, and do whatever it takes to get what belongs to me.

BECAUSE HE WAS KEEPING HIS PROMISE to the strange boy, Levi, Jay was sitting in the cemetery below Groote Schuur Hospital early on a Sunday morning. The sun had not yet risen over the distant Hottentots Holland Mountains, and a whitewashed moon was slowly fading away into a deepening blue sky. The earth was preparing itself for another hot Cape day.

The visit to his uncle had revived memories that Jay had forgotten, and which were rising like phantoms he felt he would prefer not to know.

Jay watched Levi wandering through the rows of graves.

What are you looking for so earnestly, Levi, so early in the morning?

Jay glanced up at the beatifically smiling stone face of the angel against which he leaned.

I'm looking for some answers myself. You can't give me any help, can you? No, I didn't think so. You have your own duty to attend to: the remains of Lieutenant John Markan, beloved of his wife, Martha, lie safe under your watchful gaze.

"When I die, I want to be buried here," Levi called suddenly, having stopped before a particular gravestone.

"Sorry, old chap, but that berth is already taken."

"Then it must be next door."

"Levi, this cemetery has been closed for years. There's no more room for dead people."

Jay wearily got up and walked over to where Levi was standing. Last night, before he had been allowed to escape to his room, he had had to deal with his mother's prepara-

42

tions for her evening date, hold a stilted conversation about South African politics with Brian, her boyfriend, when he arrived, and protect the family silver from his grandmother, who was still hungry. He had not slept well.

"And anyway I didn't bring you here to pick out your grave. You've got a long way to go before you end up down there, Lee."

Levi looked up at Jay and slowly shook his head.

"People can die anytime. I'm just making sure you know that's where I want to go."

The boy pointed at the small grave of David Leviticus Howard, first beloved son of Mary and Craig Howard, 1920–1929. Above the grave was a stone statue of a young boy looking seriously out on the world. In his arms he held a cat. His face had a gentle melancholy about it. Jay noticed the statue was about the same height as Levi. The two boys seemed to be looking steadily at each other.

"I don't want a cement statue, though," Levi said, staring hard at the impassive face of David Leviticus Howard.

"Hey, old man, this is getting creepy. How did you know about this chap?"

"From over there," Levi said, pointing behind him to the road that ran parallel to the cemetery. "I couldn't see the writing, and whenever I wanted to come Jenny wouldn't let me."

"Well, now that you've seen it, let's go. Hey, I've got a question for you. 'Peter, Peter, Pumpkin Eater . . .' How does it finish?"

Levi looked up at Jay in exasperation. His expression was one of determined patience, and when he finally spoke, his tone was that of a parent talking to a small child.

" 'Peter, Peter, Pumpkin Eater, had a wife and couldn't keep her. He put her in a pumpkin shell and there he kept her very well.' "

" 'Had a wife and couldn't keep her,' " Jay repeated.

"Are we finished here, then?" he asked Levi.

The boy nodded. They went over to the hole Jay had made in the fence to get into the cemetery.

"I think so too. The sun's coming up, and we don't want to be caught on private property. Anyway, I want to ask you a big favor, old man."

Levi's serious face broke into a wide smile, which vanished as quickly as it had come when he caught sight of Jay's expression.

"It hasn't got something to do with my mother, has it?" he asked suspiciously, climbing through the fence.

Jay laughed.

"No, it's got nothing to do with her. This is a real favor."

The smile returned to the boy's face as he waited for Jay to climb through and bend back the wire to hide the hole. They started walking down the road.

"A real favor," Levi repeated thoughtfully.

"You know the family that has moved into number sixteen, the black family? I can't pronounce their name— Malasuka?"

"Masakela," Levi corrected.

"Yes, that's right. Well, I've seen you talking to their son. In fact, you're the only person I've seen talking to that family at all.

"Lungile."

"What did you say?"

"His name is Lungile, and he's going to Observatory High next year. He has to do Standard Eight over again. He's from Langa and his father's a doctor at the hospital. His mother works as a clothes buyer for Woolworth."

"Wow! How did you find all that out?"

"By talking to him," Levi said, frowning at the stupidity of Jay's question.

"Oh, yes, of course. But listen, here's the favor: I want you to introduce me to him."

"Why?"

"Why! Because you know him and I don't. That's what people do for each other."

"Why?"

"Levi, don't get smart. I just want to meet him."

Jay tried to avoid the probing, old eyes of Levi—the swelling around the left one had subsided slightly—but there was no escaping the boy's scrutiny.

You always do this to me, old man. You're never satisfied with just the facts; you want to know all the details.

"Okay, okay! And stop looking at me like that. I want to meet him, because I want him to help me with something."

"What?"

"Levi! You're impossible! Just something."

Levi continued to look solemnly at Jay, waiting for him to continue.

"Okay, okay, I need to go into Khayelitsha and get a box from a man there. I don't know who else to ask, and I've never gone to a township before."

"Will you take me with you?"

"Don't be bloody ridiculous! No way! It's dangerous!"

Anger flashed in Levi's face. He stopped dead, bent down, grabbed a piece of brick that was lying in the gutter, and dashed across the empty road toward the Links Pharmacy. Too late Jay realized what the boy was planning to do.

The window!

"Levi!"

"I'll do it. I will!"

Levi, his face flushed and his small body shaking with

anger, stood poised before the plate-glass window of the pharmacy, holding the brick, ready to throw.

"Levi, put that brick down!"

"I'll do it! You know I will," Levi shouted back across the road.

"No, Levi! Listen to me. I'll take you with me."

"You've said that before, and you haven't! You're a liar! You always say things you don't mean!"

"Levi! Will you listen!"

"I will! I promise I'll throw it!"

"We'll go together. Now put that brick down!" Jay called desperately as he began cautiously to walk across the road toward the boy.

"You promise a real promise?"

"I promise!"

"Say it! Say it!"

"I promise a real promise."

The two stood looking at each other, and Jay saw the anger fading from Levi's eyes. Carefully the boy put the brick down against the wall. Jay didn't know who was more relieved, Levi or himself.

"You little tyke! What did you do that for?" Jay said, raising his hand as if to cuff Levi.

The boy flinched but nevertheless looked up at him defiantly. Jay dropped his hand.

"If you had just told me how important it was to you, but no, you have to threaten to heave bricks through windows."

"I would have."

"I know that, you idiot. I didn't know asking a favor from you would be such hard work."

"I'm sorry," Levi whispered and, distressed, timidly touched Jay's arm. "I do want to help you."

"I know you do, old man, but you don't have to get so intense about it. You're something else, Levi," Jay said, looking down at the fair-haired boy now walking quietly beside him. None of the hot anger he had so passionately displayed was evident any longer. He seemed exhausted by the storm that had invaded him and then disappeared as quickly as it had come.

"So do we have a deal, old man? You introduce me to Looleely—"

"Lungile."

"Whatever, and I'll take you with me. Okay?"

Jay turned to the boy and held out his hand, which Levi shook awkwardly.

"Okay, a deal," Levi said gravely and then, flushing, ran down the street and around the corner.

A stranger fish there never was than Levi Bam.

Jay walked on by himself, thinking about the new family that had recently moved into Observatory.

The only black people I know are servants. Bloody ridiculous!

He headed home for his breakfast. The sun had risen over the Hottentots Holland range of mountains, and the clouds were dispersing, revealing another perfect blue-sky day. Sunday morning in Observatory meant waking up to bacon and eggs, the Sunday papers, and a cacophony of church bells and church music. There were six churches on the block where Jay lived. Perhaps the souls living in Observatory were in particularly desperate need of saving, because there were more churches to the square mile there than anywhere else in the country. With so much righteousness in the air come Sunday no one could feel easy lying in bed late. Bells would ring from the Catholic church, the Pentecostals on the corner would sing their round of clapping choruses, and the Methodists their dolorous hymns.

Jay turned the corner onto his road and stopped short.

The white wall bordering the deserted plot on the corner of Station and Arnold roads displayed something he had never seen before. He could have sworn that it hadn't been there earlier that morning when he and Levi had walked past on their way to the cemetery.

Painted on the wall in bright red was bold new graffiti. Jay crossed the street and touched a letter: A smear of red came off on his finger.

GH-MK. *Must be the name of a new Salt River gang. I've not heard of it before. But there's something . . . GH-MK . . . ?*

When Jay arrived home the Turkish masseur and book-binder, Mr. Lottee, was rubbing his mother's feet. It was Margaret's Sunday-morning ritual indulgence, and she was lying on the couch, her head thrown back, her eyes shut, her dressing gown tucked around her shins, and her feet in Mr. Lottee's lap. In the corner his grandmother was sedately knitting.

Nobody looked up at Jay when he came in through the door.

"You're up early, Jay," Margaret said.

"Morning, Mr. Lottee. How are the twin souls of my mother?"

"Fine, just fine," Mr. Lottee said, nodding and smiling at Jay. He wore loose-fitting clothes to hide his rotund shape, and a floppy beige hat, which he never took off. He was really too short to be perceived as an ordinary adult man of fifty-five. The most outstanding feature of this South African of Turkish origin, aside from his lack of height, was his facial hair. He had an elegant black moustache with points beautifully waxed and twirled, sharp enough to thread through a needle. The two points stood up like miniature rugby posts on either side of his bulbous nose. His beard was fuzzed to the stiff texture of a new pot scourer and traveled all the way up to behind his ears. The moustache and beard were fastidiously groomed and so dominant that only on a closer look did one notice the two large brown eyes with a slight oriental slant set deep in his moon face.

"You have a headache, Mrs. Watson? I can feel it in your arch," Mr. Lottee said as he massaged her small feet. His broad hands were those of a larger man and could have belonged to a woodcutter or a blacksmith, but his soft palms, long fingers, and immaculately manicured fingernails were the hallmarks of a masseur.

"A sure sign of a good time last night," Jay said, and immediately regretted the sarcastic edge to his voice.

Margaret opened her eyes.

"Now, Jason, let's try to be a little civil first thing on a Sunday morning. As it so happens, Brian and I had a fabulous time. I was just telling Mr. Lottee all about it."

"And most pleasing, listening to your adventures, Mrs. Watson."

Okay, Jay-o, calm down. Don't get worked up so early in the day. Be nice. Be nice!

"How are you this morning, Grandma?"

The old woman looked up from her knitting.

"Quite well, Jason, quite well. Very nice of you to ask." She smiled at Jay, nodded, and then returned to her knitting.

"Last night I spoke to Brian about the van . . . Jason, are you listening to me?"

Jay had left the living room for the kitchen, where he had begun getting his breakfast.

"You were saying something about Brian the Bozo, and I switched off," Jay shouted.

"Jason, you're impossible!"

"Now, now. You're getting tense, Mrs. Watson. I can feel it in your heel."

"Of course I'm getting tense! With my son around it's hard not to. Ouch! Please be a little more gentle, Mr. Lottee, you seem to have found a tender spot."

49

Oh brother, me mum and her tender spots!

Jay poured himself some cereal, kicked open the kitchen door, and went out into the small backyard to eat his breakfast in the morning sun. As he sat down he saw a pair of hairy legs sticking out from under the old van, which filled most of the backyard.

Oh no! It's not Brian the Beau! My Sunday morning is developing from bad to worse to bloody awful. Is there no peace anywhere in this house?

"My dad can be a jerk sometimes," said the owner of the legs.

It's the son of the beau. The humble, apologetic, monosyllabic giant. What is my mother up to?

Jay watched the pair of legs disappear under the van and the head of Andy le Roux appear above it on the other side. He was a tall, gangly teenager, with thin, dirty blond hair hanging down around a face covered with acne. He smiled tentatively at Jay and came out from behind the van. His hands were black with grease, and oil had smudged his T-shirt, which sported the logo of a heavy metal rock band by the name of Screaming Fetus.

"I didn't mean to be rude about your father."

"That's okay. That's fine—really," Andy said, looking down dismally at Jay, who was sitting. "Your carburetor is blocked and you need a new piston head. Probably a couple of shock absorbers too."

"What the hell do you think you're doing?"

Jay put down his cereal bowl, stood up, and walked over to the van—the one that his grandfather had used to start his pet shop business.

"You don't know?" Andy said, startled by Jay's angry tone. "I thought your mother told you."

"My mother never tells me anything she thinks is good for me. And then it always comes as a nasty surprise."

"What a train smash! I thought you knew. I'm sorry, I wouldn't have touched her if I'd known. I'm sorry man, really, I'm sorry."

Andy hastily put down the carburetor he was holding as if it were a precious jewel.

Her! What is this bozo talking about? Mother, I could kill you!

Jay had met Brian's son only once before. Margaret had insisted that Jay attend a Sunday lunch at her boyfriend's house. Jay had sat on the patio by the pool and held a stilted conversation with a painfully shy boy called Andy. After an interminable afternoon of burnt sausages and soggy salad he had sworn never to go to his mother's boyfriend's house again.

"Mother!" Jay yelled into the house. Margaret appeared at the kitchen door.

"There's no need to shout, Jason," she said, walking over to them. "Jason, you remember Andy?"

"I remember Andy, Ma. What I don't remember is asking for the van to be fixed by anyone."

Andy flushed and looked around for something on which to wipe his hands, finally resorting to his T-shirt.

"Now, Jason, be reasonable. I know your grandfather left the van to you, but since your father was running it before he deserted us, and you know how much—"

"I know what you thought. But I want the van kept just the way Dad left it. Call me perverse, but that's the way I want it. Anyway, it will cost far too much to get it back on the road, and it'll never pass the roadworthy test."

"I know where to get cheap secondhand parts, and I have a friend who works at the roadworthy office," Andy interjected, looking apologetically at Jay. Jay glared at him.

Shut up, string bean! Who asked you anything?

51

At Andy's words Margaret turned triumphantly to her son. "There, you see. That's the right attitude to have. You could learn something from Andy, Jason."

Mr. Lottee appeared in the doorway, and from behind him the old woman looked out to see what all the fuss was about.

"I think a van that's working wouldn't be too bad," Mr. Lottee said, munching some of the endless supply of nuts he kept in his trouser pockets.

"He's just like Chuck. My husband would never fix the van properly," Nana said.

Jay, as usual feeling outnumbered by the women in his family, sighed heavily.

Give up, Jay-o. You know you can't win.

"Look, I don't care what you do with the old jalopy. Do what you like. I'm leaving."

With that he opened the side gate and stalked out of the backyard, banging the gate behind him.

Too late, after his dramatic exit from the backyard, Jay remembered that Bob Lo did not allow him into the hatchery on Sundays. He had nowhere else to go, so he quickly went around to the front of the house and up the stairs to his attic bedroom before the others could come in from the backyard.

Like a fish, he disliked confrontation. Once in water among rainbows and the light touching of fish fins he was fine, but his response to unwelcome reality was to lock his door and begin cutting his hair. He snipped away, cutting the strands that dangled around his ears, snipping at his fringe. He could hear his mother outside, pleading with Andy to stay.

"He'll be so pleased with you when it works. You'll see. Please don't go!"

"I don't know, Mrs. Watson. I just don't know. If he doesn't want her touched . . . I just don't know."

52

"Well, just finish what you've started. You can't leave her like that, now can you?"

There was a pause in the conversation outside, and Jay's curiosity pulled him away from the mirror over to the window. He watched Andy shrug helplessly and go back to the van.

Snip-snip, clip-clip away at those stubborn little hellions!

Soon Jay was ready to face the world again. With his hair considerably shorter, he felt renewed. He waited for his family to leave for church before he set out again. As he walked through the quiet house he pulled out the card his uncle had given him the previous day and glanced at the words written on it. The Xhosa words looked foreign on the paper. He'd never heard of Lingelethu, but it must be part of the township. He stuffed the card back into his pocket.

He heard Andy tinkering with the van in the backyard, but he was too embarrassed to go around to talk to him.

No good going back and starting a conversation with the Humble Giant. You've blown that one, Jay-o. If I want the van to lie there rotting, that should be good enough for anyone. I don't need to give reasons.

Jack Watson had promised to hand over the van to his son as soon as he acquired his own transportation. He had driven the van into the ground but had also promised his son he would fix it when he had time and money. Because he had left, there was neither time nor money, and so, when the old man died, Jay had inherited an old van that would never run again.

Jay walked down the street in the direction of Lungile's house. At the corner of the road he spotted Levi, sitting on a wall talking to Lungile inside the garden of number 16. Their heads were close together; they seemed to be sharing confidences.

What kind of courage did it take to jump out of a tank of black angels and join a tank of albino tiger fish? The laws may have been changed, but fish are fish, and they still tend to eat one another.

Jay walked up to the two.

Lungile straightened up and looked at Jay. He was about sixteen, tall, with a guarded expression.

"Hi! Welcome to the mad, mad world of Gordon Road, Observatory," Jay said self-consciously.

Both Levi and Lungile eyed him carefully. Only when he smiled did they offer him their smiles in return.

"It's only a joke. It's just the way I think of it sometimes, probably because my family's so weird."

You're talking too much, Jay-o. Shut up for a minute!

"Jason, this is Lungile," Levi said, pronouncing the African name deliberately and slowly for Jay's benefit, a hint that didn't go unnoticed by Jay.

"Hello, Lungile," he said carefully, holding out his hand across the wall that divided them.

"Hello, Jason," Lungile said with a grin, imitating the careful way Jay had just pronounced his name. Levi and Lungile grinned at each other, as if they were sharing a secret joke. Confused, Jay smiled tentatively, not understanding what it was they'd found funny.

"Levi says you want to go into Khayelitsha?"

"Yes, I have to pick up something from this address," Jay said, pulling out the card and handing it across the wall to Lungile.

"I don't know this address, but I do know where Lingelethu is. How are you going to get there?"

"I thought I'd take a taxi. You know, the ones that go up and down Main Road." Jay paused as Lungile frowned. "That's not a good idea?"

"You don't know about the taxi war?"

"I've read something about it and seen a little on television, but no, I don't know a lot about it."

"People are afraid to ride the taxis these days, especially to Khayelitsha. There really is a war going on. It's between two taxi companies, and many people have been killed. Gangsters from one taxi company stop a taxi from the other company and shoot its driver and passengers. Our neighbor's son was killed two weeks ago. He was a university student."

Lungile's words opened up an unknown, distant world to Jay. It was as if he saw only through a crack in a door, but he glimpsed something about which he had been entirely ignorant.

"I went to his funeral, and after his death nobody in my area would go by taxi. You ride with death if you take a taxi."

"Sometimes you know, and it never happens. Sometimes you never know, and then it happens," said Levi enigmatically.

Puzzled, Lungile and Jay both looked at the boy.

"That student. Your friend, Lungile. The one who's dead."

"Oh yeah," they said simultaneously, nodding, but still without understanding Levi's cryptic statement.

Lungile's words had brought an awareness of violence and death into the quiet, comfortable suburb of Observatory. Jay asked, "So how do people get to work? How do they get out of the township?"

"A lot of them don't go out, but stay at home. Those who have to go either take the bus or hitch a ride with a friend. Some even walk. They find ways. They'll lose their jobs if they don't."

Sorry, Boss. I couldn't come to work today, no taxi. Sorry worker, I've got to fire you, no work done. Out on the sand dunes thirty kilometers from the city, how do you get anywhere?

"So how am I going to get there? Can I catch a bus?"

"Not to Lingelethu, only to Khayelitsha; then you would have to walk a long way. And that wouldn't be a good idea. Don't you have a car?"

"No, I don't," Jay said, frustrated by the difficulties involved in what he'd thought would be so simple.

The Humble Giant with hairy legs! If only he hasn't left yet . . .

"Wait a moment! Come with me! Come on!" Jay said excitedly and turned to run back up the road. Levi scrambled down off the wall; Lungile came through the garden gate.

"Come on!"

The three ran up Gordon Road and burst through the gate into the Watson backyard, where Andy was washing the grease off his hands. The van was just as it had been before Andy had started working on it. All the tools had been packed away.

"Andy, you haven't stopped, have you?" Jay asked breathlessly.

Andy paused in his washing. He looked in astonishment at Jay's flushed face, at the small boy peering out from behind Jay, and then at Lungile hovering at the gate.

"Come in," Jay called to Lungile. "Andy, this is Levi and Loo . . ."

"Lungile," Levi prompted.

"Lungile," Jay finished. "Levi and Lungile, this is Andy. And he's going to get this van up and running, and we're going to take it into Khayelitsha."

"Are you serious, man?" Andy said, perplexed by Jay's sudden change of mind.

"Andy, I've never been more serious in my life, and Lungile over here is going to take us there. I'm sorry, Lungile, I haven't asked you, and I don't even know you, but will you? You see, my grandfather died a couple of months ago, and he left me this box made of yellowwood, and I have to get it. I don't know what's in it, but my grandfather left something to me, and I have to find out what it is." Jay felt he wasn't expressing himself very well as he faced the three boys, who were looking curiously at him. "It's just something I feel I have to do. I don't know why, but I *have* to do it."

"I'd like to help you, Jason," Lungile said.

"Ja, me too. Whatever you say, man. She's a good old bus, and I'd like to try to get her going," Andy said, grinning. He picked up the toolbox and opened it, preparing to start work again immediately.

"Come and look inside, you guys. There's plenty of space for everyone," said Jay.

He opened the sliding door of the van, and they all peered into the dim interior. The seats had been taken out, and cages of various shapes and sizes filled every available space along the sides, leaving a narrow alley down the middle. Behind the two front seats were larger cages that could be used as seats for human passengers. A sunroof had been crudely cut into the top of the van. The boys climbed in, and with a bit of effort Lungile managed to force open the roof. Jay opened the back door and unfolded a collapsible table that was attached to the door of the van.

"Before my grandfather ran the biggest pet shop in Cape Town, he used this van for selling his animals. He could fit a hundred different animals into the back. Look, this is where he put the pigeons, and these smaller cages were for the hamsters, mice, rats, and snakes. Down here he kept the larger puppies, and across from them were the cats. On this table he clipped parrots' wings, gave puppies injections, and groomed dogs. This van was his home before he stopped traveling and bought the pet shop. He was very proud of this van."

"My grandfather hates me," Levi said brightly. "He called me a bastard, and I don't see him anymore."

57

"Well, thanks for that bit of cheery information, old man. Just what we needed to know," said Jay, nonplussed. "So what do you think, Andy? Can you fix her?"

"Like I said, the carburetor is blocked, but I think I can clean it. You'll need some new spark plugs, an oil change, and maybe a new battery. You'll probably need a new set of shock absorbers and—"

"Hey, Andy, slow down! I'm not exactly made of money. I don't want a completely new van, I just want this one fixed up."

"My father has a spare car battery that I think we can use. I'll ask him," Lungile said, speaking up for the first time.

"Great! All right, let's start cleaning it out. It stinks of rat droppings. You want to help, Lungile?"

Lungile nodded and disappeared into the back of the van.

"Levi, go into the house and get some of the cleaning stuff under the sink. Bring some rags too. Okay, Andy, what can I help you with?"

Jay knew it would take several weeks before the van would be in running order. What with studying for his final examinations, the last days of his school career, Christmas, and New Year, he knew there would be little chance to go back to the fish tank while he had this new endeavor to occupy his mind. The box had to be found. It was a source. It held a secret.

QUEST

"THE ANSWER IS STILL NO!"

"I get this far, I do everything you want me to do, I pass my exams with flying colors, fix the old van, and then when I need to see how she runs, you won't let me."

"You haven't got a license, Jason."

"Since when have you been so law-abiding? I've got my learner's license, and that's good enough. Ma, I've graduated from school now. I'm a responsible adult, remember?"

"I don't want to discuss it anymore, Jason. And anyway, why do you want to go to Somerset West?"

"Because the roads are wide, and there's not a lot of traffic, and it will make a good test-drive. Please, Ma."

"No!"

"Thanks, Ma. That's just great!"

"Don't you raise your voice with me, young man!"

"But Ma, you're being damned unreasonable!"

"I will not have swearing in this house, Jason!"

"That's not swearing! If you want to hear swearing, I'll show you swearing."

"Jason, go to your room immediately!"

Mr. Lottee and his big hands!

"What if I asked Mr. Lottee to drive us out to Somerset West?" he asked, halfway up the stairs to his room, surprised by the idea that had suddenly struck him.

Margaret hesitated. She was unable to deny the reasonableness of his request.

"Well, I suppose that might be all right."

Pressing home his advantage, Jay bounded back down the stairs. "I know he'd love to help, and he's always wandering around by himself. He'd be perfect! I'll go and ask him."

"Jason . . ." Margaret called after him as he rushed past her and the door.

"Bye, Ma, tell Andy and Levi I'll be back in a minute!" he called, slamming the front door.

"He's just like his grandfather," Margaret muttered to herself, as she walked through the kitchen to deliver Jay's message to the boys working in the backyard.

The old van was ready! It stood in the Watson backyard looking as good as new. The canary yellow was possibly a little dazzling, but it had needed a paint job. Andy had worked wonders with the engine, and although it wheezed and coughed every now and then, the van still had quite a few kilometers left. They had fixed up the inside. The torn upholstery on the front seats had been patched over with electrical tape, and they'd mounted a crude music system in the dashboard. The sunroof had been oiled and was now working smoothly. They had left all the cages intact and used them to store spare parts, food and drink, blankets, sleeping bags, flashlights, rope, and a few other supplies.

The crowning glory was the name, which Levi had invented, and that he was painting in large letters on both side panels of the van: THE ARK.

Levi, tongue protruding, was just finishing the letter *K*. Such was his concentration that he was unaware of the red smears all over his face, nose, and arms.

He stopped painting and looked over his shoulder, first to one side and then the other.

"Jay?" he called.

"Jay's gone off somewhere, Lee," Andy said from under the van, where he was busy tying up the exhaust pipe with a bit of wire.

"There's someone here."

"I told you, man. They've gone to speak to that strange short guy.

61

"There's someone here," Levi insisted.

The boy tilted his head, as if listening to a very distant noise. He slowly walked around the van, stepped over Andy's legs, and then stopped. He opened the driver's door to the van and stared at the steering wheel.

"The steering wheel is moving."

"What are you talking about? It's only me, Levi. Pass me a pair of pliers, man!"

Levi climbed up onto the driver's seat and placed his hands on the moving steering wheel. It stopped. He turned the wheel, imitated the sound of a running engine, and changed gears.

"Levi! The pliers!" Andy called from under the van.

Levi climbed down, carefully shut the door of the van, and handed Andy the pliers.

"There was someone here, but he's gone now."

At that moment Jay and Lungile came through the back gate.

"It's *A* for *away!* We got a green light from Mr. Lottee," said Jay.

Levi beamed and Andy came sliding out from under the van. Lungile walked over to inspect Levi's artwork.

"Good job, Levi."

Andy coughed and wiped his hands on his T-shirt. He seemed embarrassed.

"My dad says going into the township is pretty risky," he said, avoiding looking at Lungile. "A lot of people are getting killed in the cross fire of the taxi war, and . . ." He stopped, his unspoken doubt hanging between them. They all turned to Lungile, who shifted uneasily.

"Yes, there's trouble on the streets. I know people who have been affected, and the other day someone else I knew was killed. I suppose it is dangerous, but people are still living there." Lungile paused. He seemed to be searching for the right words, and then in frustration he blurted out: "Everybody still goes to work, kids still go to school, the shops are still open. It's not as if the community has come to a stop because of the violence. I mean, you can't just abandon the place because it's got problems!"

"Nobody wants to know about where the black people live," Levi said.

"Exactly, old man!" Jay exclaimed. "We've pretended—I mean, white people have pretended—that the townships don't exist. We can't do that anymore."

Brave words, Jay-o. Meanwhile you're scared silly!

"But all we know about places like Khayelitsha is how violent they are," Andy insisted.

"The problem is, Andy, it's all you see in the newspapers and on the television, and everybody thinks the whole place is burning up, and people are living under siege," Jay responded.

"But you're not saying the violence doesn't happen, Lungile?" Andy asked.

"It can be very dangerous," Lungile said softly. "But it's not true that the whole place is burning up. That's what gives the community a bad name. Look, I think we'll be okay. We're going in the morning, and . . ." Lungile stopped and looked helplessly at them. He shrugged, and sadness seemed to overwhelm him.

Jay was alarmed by the somber mood that had settled on them all. He had to do something. He stood up and whistled a long, low note.

"It's not as if we're noticeable or anything," he said, jerking his head at the bright yellow van.

"Man, I never thought of that! We're going to stand out like a sore thumb," Andy groaned.

"That might be a good thing," Lungile said.

"Look are we going or not? Andy, I know you're worried. To be honest, I'm a little nervous too. But let's just go!"

Andy nodded. "You're right, Jason. Let's find out for ourselves."

"What if the Ark breaks down?"

"Levi!" Jay reprimanded. "We're not going to think like that! Besides, that's why Andy's coming with us. Everybody's got a job: Lungile's showing us the way, Mr. Lottee's driving, Andy's our mechanic."

"And me?"

"You're here because I made my first real promise to you, remember? You're also our mascot, Levi. You'd better bring us luck and stop saying negative things. So tomorrow it is, everyone."

I'm tracking down the yellowwood box. I'm on the trail. I have the address in my pocket. Onward, onward!

THE ARK SAILED along the N2 highway, passed the Mowbray and Rondebosch golf courses and the two cooling towers, and headed toward the purple mountains of the Hottentots Holland range. Passengers in passing cars turned to watch the bright yellow van named so boldly in red.

Inside the van, Mr. Lottee sat on two telephone books and peered over the steering wheel, watching the road, his rearview mirror, and the temperature gauge all at the same time. Next to him, Levi perched on a make-shift seat with his legs on either side of the gear lever. Like a tiny monarch with folded arms, who owned all he surveyed, he viewed the world rushing by. Behind Levi, Lungile and Andy, sitting on two large cages, looked out of the side windows. Repeatedly Andy would instruct Mr. Lottee, who paid him little attention. The sunroof was open, and it was cool inside the van. Jay was in the passenger seat with his elbow out of the open window, experiencing a sense of wonder at the fact that he was sailing down the N2 in his grandfather's old van. He was quiet and ignored Andy's running commentary on every slightest change in the engine's tone. The wind blew through his hair, which he'd allowed to grow considerably longer in the past six weeks, and he thought of Chuck Watson.

He was always so Right, with a capital R. Nothing I said could make him change his mind, even when he was as sick as he was. I want to be that sure of things. Okay, he broke Nana's heart when he left her for his ten-year walkabout. And he wasn't a good father to either of his sons or, I have to admit, even a good grandfather. Some people are just not family men. Chuck Watson certainly wasn't.

Jay no longer associated the van with his father but with his grandfather. As he'd been working on the Ark—Levi had been rather clever to name the van so well—his thoughts had turned to the last days he had spent with his grandfather. Growing up, he had heard so much about the irrepressible Chuck Watson that when a frail, old man had arrived at Gordon Road and had to be helped into the bed he would never again leave, Jay had been very disappointed. It was hard to believe that that mumbling, drooling old man had caused so much turmoil in the Watson family.

What made you special, Gramps? If anything.

Chuck Watson had left his second wife suddenly one night and had disappeared with no explanation other than a note to say that he had not committed suicide. Friends had aired their opinions of his character—"Just the sort of thing Chuck Watson would do!"—but had been unable to offer any reason for his behavior. His business colleagues, however, had noticed that Chuck had lost all enthusiasm for his work. And all the family members had had their own thoughts as to why he had abandoned them.

And then ten years later you came back. Out of the blue. After I had forgotten you and couldn't recognize the sick, old man being helped out of the taxi. You came back—why?

Chuck had returned to Cape Town when a stroke had paralyzed his left side. He had offered no explanation, either for the missing ten years or for his sudden reappearance. His daughter-in-law, Margaret, was the only one who had offered to look after him. What Jay had remembered as the rambunctious rogue of his childhood had turned into a semiparalyzed, incoherent old man. With a mixture of curiosity and fear, Jay had approached the man who had built up the largest pet shop empire in the southern hemisphere.

From his family and friends Jay had heard numerous stories about his grandfather's life: how Chuck's first wife had died in childbirth and how he had married again six months later; how he had started his business by roaming the countryside collecting animals and selling them as pets from the back of the van; how he had been given the first rights to export rhinoceros and had been thrown into jail when his license was revoked; how he had caught an elephant when that species still roamed the Knysna forest and sold it to the Boswell Wilkie circus; how he had specialized in breeding tropical fish and then engaged a young Chinese man to research a method of breeding the first neon tetras in South Africa; how he had once owned twenty Pet Emporiums throughout South Africa and, finally, how he had disappeared for ten years, leaving his business in the hands of Peter and Jack, his sons from each of his two marriages; and how they had come close to bankrupting the pet empire.

At first Jay had entered his grandfather's sickroom in trepidation. He had feared the old man's capricious moods. Some days his grandfather would be in good humor, but more often he would be crotchety or downright irascible. Jay realized that much of his moodiness had to do with his physical condition. Chuck could only move his left hand and shake his head. From his mouth came a language of grunts, which Jay learned with difficulty to interpret. However, what had initially been a chore defined by his mother as spending time with the invalid gradually became an intriguing diversion from mid-year exams and the wet winter. But just at the point when Jay had become absorbed in talking to his grandfather and learning more about his life, the old man had died.

Jay had thought he was prepared for his grandfather's

death, for the doctor had warned them it could happen at any moment. However, when death had finally come Jay had experienced a sense of profound loss, for he had discovered that trapped in his grandfather's crippled body was a vigorous and witty intellect.

The memories of the last winter with his ailing grandfather had permeated Jay's work on the Ark, and the resurrection of the old van became a dedication to Chuck Watson.

You went too soon, Gramps. You never had a chance to answer the questions I needed to ask. When you died you took with you the glimpse you had given me of another era. It was as if a window onto a town I'd never visited had been blocked off.

The Ark sailed past the airport and entered the Cape Flats. As they left Cape Town farther behind them, they saw the overflow from the townships beginning to creep up to the edges of the highway. Shanties spilled over the dunes. The structures had crude squares of corrugated iron for roofs, with cardboard or plastic for walls, and small doorways into dark interiors.

We don't go near it. We are frightened off by reports of shootings, gang violence, high crime rates. Beyond those dunes is chaos—or so we are told—and we stay away.

On either side of the highway the Port Jackson scrub was rapidly being depleted by the need for firewood to feed the hungry cooking fires. Jay could remember driving along the highway and seeing nothing but dense undergrowth. Today, however, he could see the thronging patchwork squares of shanties everywhere and, every five hundred meters, the tall industrial lights that had been erected to illuminate poverty. In the bushes some distance away from the shantytown were the black plastic-bag igloos of the young men undergoing initiation. Lungile pointed out the naked boys, with chalked bodies and white faces, who were preparing themselves for manhood and had isolated themselves from their community.

If only we had some ceremony that showed us the way into the adult world. I would gladly paint my face, leave home for three months, live off the veld, learn secret rituals, if I could be sure it would make me into a man.

"Khayelitsha, next off-ramp," said Mr. Lottee, slowing down.

He turned off the highway at the next exit and followed the blue signs to Khayelitsha. The passengers in the van were silent as they began to pass through rows upon rows of shanties. On their right, shacks spread out to the horizon; on their left were lines of small, upright cement oblongs twenty rows deep.

"What are those?" asked Jay.

"Toilets," answered Lungile. "People have to cross the road if they want to go to the toilet. The houses don't have running water. There is one public faucet to a block."

The main road running through the township was tarred, but narrower dirt tracks led into the maze of shacks on either side of it. There were double-story, brick buildings among the shanties, some of them as yet unfinished.

"And those brick buildings?"

"Those are the new schools. There aren't enough chairs, but at least now they have roofs and classrooms. When I was a junior, school used to be out in the open. We didn't get much schoolwork done. You want to turn right at the police station, Mr. Lottee."

They passed a police compound surrounded by razor wire. It looked like a fortress. Blue-uniformed men, armed with shotguns, stood at the entrance. Parked inside the compound was a beetle-shaped Casspir, an armored military vehicle used to quell rioting.

"Turn right here."

Mr. Lottee swung a sharp right, and the van left the

tarred road for a dirt track so narrow that the Ark's passengers could look straight into the front rooms of the shacks. Small children playing in the dust waved at them. An old woman sold sweets, soap, and cool drinks from a window in her shack. Another woman glanced up from sweeping the doorstep of her house. A dog ran in front of the van, and Mr. Lottee swerved to miss it.

"You'll have to slow down here. There are many accidents," said Lungile, tapping Mr. Lottee on the shoulder as the van and its passengers jolted and jarred into potholes and over ruts. They moved in a cloud of dust.

The Ark received only a few casual glances, but Jay was peering intently out of his window at women with babies strapped to their backs with blankets, people laden with plastic bags of shopping, small front rooms crammed with furniture, shacks with television antennas, people lining up for water.

"I probably sound naive, Lungile, but everything looks so normal."

"That's what I was trying to tell you back in Observatory; people go on with their lives and live with the trouble. But don't be fooled. Three blocks away I could show you where a taxi was blown apart by gunfire, and where police opened fire to stop a fight and an eight-year-old girl was killed in the cross fire. But here there is nothing."

"Where did you used to live, Lungile?" Mr. Lottee asked.

"I lived in Langa. It's one of the older townships closer to town, but I have family and friends in Khayelitsha. Many people who live here have come from the Transkei and can't find a proper place to live. We don't all live like this. Our house had three bedrooms and a garden."

"I've never seen so many houses in one block, man. This is unbelievable." Andy was standing up with his head sticking out of the sunroof.

"You must turn left at the next road."

"How do you know where you are when the roads have no names?"

"You get used to it, but I don't know where this number is. I'll have to ask."

As Mr. Lottee slowed down to turn the corner, Lungile leaned across Jay to call to a woman in the road. He spoke to her in Xhosa, and she answered him, turned, and pointed down the road.

"It's straight down and then right."

Mr. Lottee drove on, turning into the next track to the right. It would have been easy to get lost. Everything looked the same. One street was like another. Everywhere small children peeped out of narrow, squat doorways.

Is this only twenty minutes from where I live? Here homes are shacks, toilets are across the road, water is from one communal tap per block, school is a brick building without any chairs or desks.

"I'd like to live here. Everybody I've seen has a friend," said Levi, pointing to a group of children his own age playing in the dust between two shacks.

"Number thirty-nine should be around here. It might be painted on something somewhere."

Swinging around a corner, the Ark almost ran into a large crowd gathered around a cement-block house. Mr. Lottee slowed down, and the people walking toward the crowd parted to allow the van through. When the van stopped Lungile got out and waited uncertainly. People in the crowd eyed them suspiciously. Lungile spoke in Xhosa to a man walking past, who pointed at the cement-block house.

"This is number thirty-nine, but there's something wrong. These people are dressed for a funeral. Wait here, and I'll go find out what's going on."

Mr. Lottee leaned out of the driver's window as Lungile

went up to some people standing near the house and spoke to them.

The respectful silence of the gathering was suddenly broken by the sound of a loud exclamation. The crowd parted to allow Lungile and a woman dressed in black through. She seemed stocky and solidly large next to the thin boy walking beside her. On her round face was a pair of spectacles, which gave her a businesslike air. Her head was uncovered, and the white stubble was the only indication that she was over sixty. Lungile was talking excitedly to her. When she saw the van she stopped in astonishment.

"However did you know?" she said, as she came up to Jay. "Who told you?"

"I'm sorry. I don't understand," Jay said from inside the Ark.

"Are you waiting for a police escort before you get out of the van?" Lungile said with a wry smile. Jay flushed and climbed down to greet the woman.

"This is Mrs. Jacobs. She thinks you knew about her husband's death and that you have come to his funeral," Lungile said to Jay and then turned to the woman. "This is Jay Watson. He is the grandson of the man you speak of."

The woman shook her head in amazement, laughed loudly, and then enthusiastically embraced Jay. Over her shoulder she shouted to the people around the house. They came over to the van.

"Here is the grandson of the Pet Master, the man who sold us Lucky."

The people smiled at Jay as they surrounded him and greeted him. With the woman's announcement the mood of the gathering had changed; no longer did the crowd look suspiciously at the visitors. People peered into the van and some children laughed at Mr. Lottee, who was still perched on the telephone books. Levi glared at them from his seat.

72

"Arthur Jacobs is dead?" Jay asked.

Lungile turned to Mrs. Jacobs, who was inspecting the interior of the van, and spoke to her in Xhosa.

"He died early this morning," Lungile said, translating her response.

"When we heard your grandfather had passed into the other world we were very sorry," Mrs. Jacobs said to Jay.

"You knew my grandfather?"

"Yes! Yes! Of course I knew him. This is his van, but it's not the color I remember. He always came in this van when he visited us. Then we were not living here. In those days we lived in District Six. That was before the Boer moved us. Come, come inside. You must be hot. Bring your friends."

"We don't want to bother you. It's obviously not convenient for you now."

"Come, my husband won't mind. That's why all these people are here. They have come to say good-bye to him, sit and talk about him, before he leaves us finally. You are welcome to join in. You are the grandson of the Pet Master. Arthur and he were old friends."

"It is true," Lungile said. "If an old person dies, people come to talk about him and his life before he leaves the home for good."

"I want to show you what Chuck gave us. Did he ever tell you about the horse that won the Horse 'n Cart show five years running?"

Jay and Lungile followed Mrs. Jacobs through the crowd. Andy, Levi, and Mr. Lottee did not know whether to join them or not.

"Come! Bring your friends," Mrs. Jacobs called as she disappeared down the alley beside the house.

Shoved on by Lungile, Jay had no choice but to follow her.

"There, see? That's what Chuck brought my husband when there was no horse to be found."

In a small clearing at the back of the shack a shaggy old horse was tethered to a pole.

"You should have seen Lucky when we first got her. She was tall and strong, and her coat shone. But like us she's grown old."

"My grandfather gave you that horse?"

Jay's question was met with a burst of laughter from Mrs. Jacobs.

"Not gave, we paid for her. Arthur needed a horse to cart the scrap metal we collected. That was a long time ago, when work was difficult and the Boer made living impossible for us. Your grandfather met Arthur and promised him the finest horse in Africa. We thought he was just another liberal whitey, making promises he wouldn't keep. You should have seen our faces when he came back a week later in that van of his, pulling a trailer. Inside the trailer was Lucky."

Mrs. Jacobs walked over to the horse and patted the animal's neck. Mr. Lottee, Levi, and Andy, who had come up behind Lungile, also listened as the woman spoke.

"He said she had run in the Durban July. Ja, that's what he said, and we believed him. He was a good storyteller, your grandfather. Of course we didn't have enough money to pay for Lucky, but Arthur and Chuck made a deal. Arthur would pay him whenever we had spare cash, and in his rounds to pick up metal Arthur would tell people about your grandfather's pet business and get orders for him. Chuck would come at least twice a month to deliver snakes, kittens, birds—whatever people wanted. And even when Lucky was paid for, Chuck would still come round in his van filled with animals. That old van carried every animal you can imagine, and if he didn't have what you wanted you would get it the next time he came round. But business here wasn't as good as it was in District Six. Then people could still afford pets."

"Did you see Chuck before he got ill? I mean, when was the last time you saw him?" Jay asked.

"It was a long time ago, maybe a year. No, it was more like two years ago. He wasn't selling animals then. Yes, he was doing something else. He came and spoke for hours with Arthur."

So if he came to us in January last year, then the Jacobses must have seen Gramps when he was on his walkabout. Two years ago you were here, Chuck Watson, this close to home, and you didn't contact your family.

"What was he doing here?"

"Just visiting. He hadn't seen us in a long time. He still had shops then—we'd seen them in town—but he said his sons were losing his money. It was a bad thing that he had stopped working with animals, but he was happy traveling around in his van. I don't know what he was doing, but he smiled a lot, like a man who has a happy secret. He said what he was doing was more important than his old job, but we'd all hear about it soon. He would make sure of that."

More people had come down the alley to listen to Mrs. Jacobs, and the party from the van, except for Levi, had grouped themselves behind Jay. Levi had gone up to Lucky, who had lowered her head so that the small boy could stroke her forehead.

"I came to see you, Mrs. Jacobs," said Jay, "because my grandfather wanted me to have his yellowwood box. I was told that your husband bought it at an auction."

"Oh no! Don't say that!" Mrs. Jacobs threw up her hands. "I told Arthur again and again that someone would come for it one day, but he said he knew who it had to go to. I told him and told him, but would he listen to me? No!" In an angry burst of Xhosa Mrs. Jacobs spoke rapidly and at some length to the people who crowded about her.

"What's she saying?" Jay whispered to Lungile.

"Something about how her husband never listened to her and that she should have been a bossier wife," Lungile summarized, rolling his eyes at Jay.

"Mrs. Jacobs, then you haven't got the box your husband bought at the auction?" Jay asked quickly, as Mrs. Jacobs paused for breath.

"When Chuck came to visit he always had that box with him. He told us that his life was in that box. I don't know what he meant. Arthur knew what Chuck was trying to do, but he didn't tell me. That was just like my husband. He only told me what he thought I should know."

"So you don't have the box anymore?"

"No. That husband of mine—even though I told him that someone would come and pick it up—said that it must go to a woman in Mossel Bay. He wanted to take it there himself, but I wouldn't let him. He was too sick. So a few weeks ago he gave it to a friend who was going home to the Transkei."

Mossel Bay! That's five hours away. Drat and blast it all!

Jay's spirits fell as he realized he had arrived a few weeks too late to catch up with his grandfather's last gift to him. He gazed dolefully at Mrs. Jacobs, who, seeing how disappointed he was, patted him energetically in commiseration.

The passengers from the van wandered back to the front of the house and hung about, not knowing what to do next. Jay stood miserably on one side, while Mrs. Jacobs explained again and at length what had happened and how Arthur should have listened to her more often.

"So we go to Mossel Bay," said Levi staunchly. "It's just over that mountain," he said, pointing to the Hottentots Holland range.

"You're right, old man." Jay smiled down at the boy. "I guess we'll have to take the road to Mossel Bay."

Lungile came up to where Levi and Jay were standing.

76

He held a piece of paper, which he handed to Jay. "I asked her for the address of the person in Mossel Bay. You're not going to stop now. Right?" he asked.

I want to give up, go home, forget this silly wild-goose chase, but, Chuck, you intrigue me. What were you doing roaming the countryside? How come you didn't show your face to your family in Cape Town, but visited your black friends in the township? What were you up to?

"No, you're right, Lungile. I'm not going to give up yet."

They said their good-byes to Mrs. Jacobs, who continued to apologize to Jay, and climbed back into the van. Mr. Lottee reversed and then pulled out of the cul-de-sac to get back onto the tarred road. Behind them, several people waved as they drove away.

Once they reached the highway, the Ark sped back to Observatory. The shanties seemed to trail behind them for miles, and everyone was quiet.

"Lungile, I'm sorry for being so stupid yesterday. I was just scared, man," Andy said, breaking the silence.

"It's okay."

"No, I've just realized I never would have gone to Khayelitsha before, and now I'm glad I did, because now I know what it's really like. It still scares me a little, but somehow it feels different . . ." Andy said, his words trailing off.

He spoke as if he were thinking aloud, wrestling with something much larger than himself. No one had ever heard him say so much before. His confession made Jay forget for the moment about his grandfather's box. He too couldn't understand the spinning complexity of his own feelings. The problems of the community he had just visited seemed overwhelming. Nobody spoke as they finally left the last shanties behind.

When they approached Cape Town, Lungile leaned forward. "Jay, what are you going to do now?" he asked.

"Do you want to come to Mossel Bay?"

"I've never been there, so why not?"

"Andy, do you think the Ark will make it to Mossel Bay and back?"

"Ja, sure—as long as we're not in a hurry. It's a long way for such an old lady, but I think she'll make it."

"Mr. Lottee, will you drive us there?"

"Well, we'll have to see what your mother thinks about this. It will be nice to get out of Observatory for a change. If she has no objections, I'd love to have a day in the country."

"I'm coming too," Levi pitched in.

"Good, then let's leave early Monday morning, say six. We could get there about one o'clock, pick up the box, and come straight back. We should make it back to Cape Town that night. No problem, real simple."

IT WAS THE SUMMER of the disappearing blouse. Jenny Bam was experimenting with one of her designs. It had started out as a creation cut well below the hips, but as the summer progressed it gradually shrank, first revealing her belly button then increasing expanses of silky skin. The possibility that the blouse would in time entirely disappear inflamed Jay's imagination.

Try and keep your eyes on her face, Jay-o. Show a little maturity and breathe deeply.

There were times when he did wish he was older, and most of them were when he contemplated Jenny Bam. She was about ten years older than him, a Mediterranean beauty with long black hair and emerald eyes cut from the finest stone. A single parent running her own dressmaking business, she was unmistakably a female adult. Jay sometimes felt being adult could have certain advantages. He imagined himself, eloquent and sophisticated, asking Jenny Bam out for dinner. It was only a happy fantasy, since Jenny was already dating the man who drove the black truck and who had called him "kid." Nevertheless it was a fantasy that he wistfully entertained—and one that Levi liked ruthlessly to demolish.

"Jay likes your new blouse, Jenny. He told me so," the boy said slyly. They were sitting in the kitchen about to have a cup of tea. Jay, having dropped in on his way to the hatchery, had found Jenny and Levi just finishing breakfast. The sink was full of dirty dishes, and all flat surfaces in the room were covered with plates, overflowing ashtrays, dress materials, dirty coffee cups, shears, and other dressmaking equipment.

Jay turned pink with embarrassment.

"Thank you, Jay. I haven't finished it yet, but I'm hoping to get this range ready for next summer. It still needs a little more work."

"I think it's great the way it is," Jay said, and blushed a deeper shade of red as Jenny twirled around the kitchen table, showing off her garment, to open the refrigerator door.

"Oh no! We're out of milk. Levi, won't you be a honey and run down to Zitties for a liter? Oh, don't look so grumpy. It won't take you long."

Levi reluctantly got up, glaring at both his mother and Jay.

"Oh, Levi! Wipe off that frown. You're always so fierce about everything," said Jenny Bam, ruffling the boy's hair. Levi dodged his mother's hand.

"Why don't you ask her and get it over with," he muttered to Jay.

"Levi is always so grumpy in the mornings. Now don't try your stare on me, my boy. It won't work. Come on, here's the money, and make it snappy. The kettle's boiled already." Jenny dismissed her son, who was still scowling at her as he left the room.

Jenny watched the small boy go down the passage, sighed, and then turned back to Jay. "He's not an easy child. Thanks for putting up with his nonsense. Very few people do. Did he tell you what happened at school the other day?"

"He said his teacher shouted at him and he was sent home early."

"He sneaked out my dressmaking scissors and gouged huge chunks out of his desk, and then cut up his textbook into small pieces. He threatened the teacher with the scissors when she tried to take them away from him. She says she's scared of him. She doesn't want him in her class any-more."

"No, he didn't tell me that."

"I didn't think he would. He lies a lot. It's something I can't stand. I think he does it just to make me angry. Sometimes I get so mad with him it's hard to think straight. Do you know what I mean?"

She had dropped her voice, as if she were discussing something secret with Jay. He wasn't sure how to answer, so he nodded and covered his confusion by changing the subject.

"He did a great job painting the Ark. He took it very seriously."

"He likes you, Jay." Jenny smiled.

I don't know if I want that honor. It sounds more like a responsibility. You sound like an adult discussing a child, Jay-o. Listen to the words coming from your mouth.

"Levi's okay," Jay said, uncomfortable at the personal turn the conversation had taken and feeling somehow disloyal to the boy.

"He's got such a terrible temper. It suddenly flares up from nowhere. Jay, do you know that Levi is on medication?"

"No, I didn't know that."

"He's a hyperactive child and has trouble concentrating for any length of time. The doctor suggested we put him on Ritalin. It's some kind of depressant, but then sometimes he gets so low he becomes quite uncontrollable."

This is a nine-year-old boy we're talking about!

"I don't deal with his temper very well. Neither does Gary. That's my boyfriend. I think you've met him?"

"Yes, I have." Jay recalled the tall man in a brown leather jacket, stepping out of a truck and hugging Jenny. A twinge of jealousy accompanied the image as Jay remembered how

Jenny had introduced him to Gary and disappeared into the cottage arm in arm with her boyfriend.

"But here I am waffling on about my problem child and you want to ask me something."

"I wanted to ask you whether Levi could come with us to Mossel Bay on Monday? I'm going to see someone, and I sort of promised Lee he could tail along. We'll leave early Monday morning and come back that night."

"I don't know, Jay. Levi hasn't been behaving very well lately, and he has to take his medication. Are you sure you want to have so much responsibility?"

"He's been a great help in getting the van on the road."

Let it go, Jay-o, if she doesn't want to, let it go. Why are you pushing so hard for the old man?

"Yes, he told me about naming that van of yours. You say you'll be away all day Monday?"

"Yes."

Jenny thought for a moment.

"What time do you think you'll be back?"

"Probably about seven or eight o'clock."

"Good! That means Gary and I can go sailing all day."

"We'll be going with Mr. Lottee, so you don't need to worry."

"That creepy little fellow I see walking up and down Station Road?"

"Jenny, you are rude. Mr. Lottee is not creepy. He is small, like me," Levi said angrily, appearing suddenly in the doorway.

"Huh oh! Look who's back! The voice of reason. Now don't get touchy, Levi." Jenny looked at Jay. "He's like that whenever I talk about anyone short. He'll probably be a dictator one day. You know what they say about short people," she said, turning to her son while she poured the tea. He scowled back at her and banged the milk bottle down on the table.

"It's rude to talk like that about people. Isn't it, Jay?"

"Levi, don't start your nonsense again," Jenny warned.

Time to make a speedy exit, Jay-o. You don't want to get caught in the cross fire.

"So what do you think, Jenny?"

"I don't see why anybody would want to be around crabby Levi, but if you want to take him with you I don't mind."

Addressing Levi, who had gone to stand next to the seated Jay, she smiled a threat. "And you, monster, you stay out of trouble between now and then, or else you're not going. You hear me? I mean it."

Levi met her eyes and nodded. A temporary truce seemed to be in place between them. Looking at them—the small, solemn, fair-headed boy with the fierce eyes and the young, vivacious, dark-haired woman with the warm smile—Jay found it hard to believe they were mother and son.

Children come from you, but they don't belong to you. How did you come from her, old man?

Jay stood up and, stealing one more glance at Jenny Bam's belly button, hastily retreated to the door.

"Well, thanks for the tea, and I'll see you later, Lee."

"I'm coming with you."

"Oh no, you're not," said Jenny quickly. "You're staying here and helping me clean up this mess. Gary's coming round and he wants to go to the beach."

"I don't want to go to the beach. I don't want to be with Gary either."

"Levi, you will do as I say. Holding your breath isn't going to make me change my mind, so don't try that one on me."

"I'll catch up with you later, old man. I've got to go and see Bob Lo," Jay called to Levi as he escaped down the passage to the front door.

"We have to keep looking for it, Jay," Levi called from the kitchen doorway.

"You bet! We will, Lee. We will!" said Jay, as he opened the front door and left the cottage.

Whew! Glad to get out of that pressure cooker!

Jay walked up Fish Alley and thought about mothers. He felt a tinge of remorse for the way he often treated his own mother. Usually he didn't understand where his anger came from. As with Levi, it often seemed to come from nowhere. It flared suddenly, and he recognized with shame that it was frequently triggered by a cause that must have appeared extremely childish to any onlooker. He remembered some of the painful exchanges he had recently had with his mother. Most of them had had to do with Brian the Beau. He had to admit she didn't date many men. In fact, if he were to be absolutely honest, Brian was the first man whom she had been seeing regularly since his father had left a year ago.

Would I rather be a mother or a father, I wonder? I push my mother away, scratch at her, bite her, hurt her if she comes near. It can't be pleasant for her. Maybe fathers don't feel the same way as mothers. Obviously mine doesn't—cruising around Africa on his motorbike with his baby glued to his back. The Watson men stink. The Watson women are batty. It's as simple as that.

At the end of Fish Alley he unlocked the gate to Bob Lo's hatchery and went into the house.

"Bob!" he called as he walked down the cluttered passage. The house was silent. As he went through the kitchen he called again.

"I'm in here! There's no need to blooming shout like that," Bob Lo called from the office. "I'm working on something very delicate at the moment, and your shouting doesn't help matters."

84

Bob Lo was leaning over a small tank on his desk, knitting needle in one hand and forceps in the other. "I think I may have the start of a new species here," he said excitedly.

Swimming idly about in the tank was a solitary goldfish. Across the top of the tank lay a large magnifying glass, which enlarged the fish whenever it swam into its shadow.

"Look, see the heart-shaped scales. Aren't they perfect? Look! Of course the color is a bit off, not a brilliant enough orange, just a little too pale. But I'm getting closer. Can you see the potential there, Jay? Those are good genes I can use."

Some things never change. Bob, there is a life beyond your fishes.

"Bob, tell me about my grandfather. How did you meet him? You've never told me."

"Will you look properly? I think we could be on to something here."

Jay stared through the magnifying glass and tried to see what was making Bob Lo so excited. He didn't notice anything different. In fact, they looked like ordinary goldfish.

"You've never asked me before."

"Huh?" Jay glanced up from the magnifying glass.

"Your grandfather. You never asked about him before."

"Well, I've never been interested before. Now it's different. I'm finding out things about him that are puzzling. Those ten years he disappeared he didn't go very far. In fact he was in Khayelitsha a couple of years ago. Everybody thought he'd left the country, but he hadn't. I think he spent some time in Mossel Bay too. Rather than come home to his family, he was visiting friends in the township, people I've never heard of before. I don't understand why he did that."

Bob Lo studied Jay for a moment and put the knitting

needle and forceps on the table. He pulled open his desk drawer and, muttering, shuffled among the papers.

"Now where did I put it! I could have sworn it was here. Sit down, Jay, sit down." Jay sat down. "Ah, here it is!"

Bob Lo handed Jay a black-and-white photograph. In it Jay saw two young men standing in front of a familiar, but very new, sign:

BOB LO'S TROPICAL FISH
EMPORIUM
SAT 10-5
CLOSED ON SUNDAYS

One of the men in the photograph was a young, casually dressed Chuck Watson, who had his arm around the shoulders of a thin, solemn Chinese man wearing a dark suit. Chuck was beaming, apparently in high spirits, but the Chinese man, unsmiling, appeared embarrassed by his companion's show of affection and looked ill at ease posing for the camera.

"Is that you with a moustache?"

"Who else did you think it was?"

Bob Lo, a Chinese Clark Gable. You handsome devil, you!

"But you look so different. Why are you so serious?"

"Because your grandfather had insisted on taking a photograph to celebrate selling his tropical fish business to me, and I was nervous about the photograph getting into the newspapers."

"Why?"

"You're certainly full of questions today. Why don't you just shut up and let me speak. I must think a moment."

Bob Lo moved out from behind his desk, cleared some books off his chair, and sat down facing Jay.

"My father came to South Africa in 1900. He thought he was going to get rich quickly here. That's a family joke now! The government was shipping people in from China to work in the mines, and many Chinese came to South Africa to escape the war at home. The government called the men cheap labor, but they were nothing more than slaves. Anyway, they were given a five-year contract, and when the five years were over they were to be shipped back to China. Finished and *klaar!*" Bob Lo smacked his hands together for emphasis.

"My father decided not to go back to China. He thought he would have a better chance in this country than in his own and decided to run away from Johannesburg with my mother. They escaped to Kimberley, and that's where I grew up. When I was nineteen I applied to the University of Cape Town to study medicine. That's another family joke. The university authorities thought my surname was Afrikaans—they thought it was spelled L-O-U-W. When I arrived at the university and they saw I was Chinese, they said there had been a mistake and that I couldn't live in a residence or study at their university. Ja, they didn't know what to do with a Chinese South African. They had no bloody box to put me into."

Bob Lo got up and paced around the room. Glancing again at the photograph, Jay noticed that Bob Lo had actually not changed very much from the serious man in the snapshot.

"But you quickly learn how to work the system when you have to. I learned something from the Boer: I wrote away for a correspondence course and used the name *Louw* to get myself passed off as an Afrikaner. I decided not to go back to Kimberley. I liked Cape Town, but in order to survive I needed to get a job, and in those days it wasn't easy. That was how I met Chuck Watson. Look at the photograph. You said I seemed a very serious young man. And I was, very serious. I carried the biggest chip on my shoulder, and I was angry most of the time. Man, in those days I was a bloody second-class citizen. I was not black, and I was not white. So I was classified as Asian, even though I

87

was born in Kimberley. It was ridiculous and didn't make any sense. Your grandfather taught me how to laugh at the system, and he gave me my first job."

Jay looked again at the photograph. He tried to imagine the two young people he saw there, frozen in black and white, moving around in color talking to each other.

"When was that?"

"I met your grandfather in 1951, and, man, was South Africa a crazy place to live in then! I was a little older than you are now, maybe twenty or twenty-one. Angry, shooo, so bloody angry, I couldn't think straight. I couldn't get any decent work because nobody wanted to hire a 'Chink'! Your grandfather had just bought a new van and was setting up his pet business. He was a whitey, you see, so he could apply for loans from the bank and register himself as a legitimate business."

"How old was my grandfather when you met him?"

"I think he must have been twenty-five, not much older than me. I was walking down Main Road, and I saw this steel gray van parked on the corner. A crowd had gathered around the back of the van, and a man in a suit was selling parrots, fish, hamsters, snakes, crickets—"

"Crickets!" Jay said.

"Cricket runs were big in those days. People would gamble on how fast a cricket could run down a track. Lots of pay packets were lost on Friday afternoons on the cricket runs in Salt River and Observatory. Well, I knew a little about tropical fish because my father kept some and had taught me how to breed them. So I talked to your grandfather and he gave me the job of collecting fish, cleaning out tanks—just like the work you do for me. But I had something special that made me very valuable to your grandfather," Bob Lo said proudly, and paused.

Jay could hear his grandfather's voice again, and dimly he remembered the vitality of the man he had briefly known ten years ago when he was a seven-year-old boy.

"I could get rare types of tropical fish from China despite the ban on pet trading with other countries. I made friends with the Chinese sailors who came to Cape Town, and offered them money, food, or whatever they wanted if they would bring me tropical fish from the East. They would come off the ships carrying those billy cans they used for lunch. In the bottom half of the billy there would be a rare kind of tropical fish. Your grandfather gave me a commission on every fish I smuggled into the country. And that's how I got enough money to buy the tropical fish business from him."

"You were able to buy the tropical fish business with the money you made from commissions?"

Bob Lo flushed at the question and looked at Jay irritably.

"It doesn't matter where I got the money from. I got it and I bought the tropical fish part of Chuck's pet empire. By then he had shops all over the country and he was getting too big. He was glad to sell off that part of the business. He'd changed, and he wasn't so interested in animals anymore. He wanted other things in life. I'd changed, too, and I'd found what I wanted to do. I wanted to discover how to breed new species of goldfish, and so I stopped studying medicine and went into tropical fish."

Why does my job at the hatchery interest me no longer? All I see are fish swimming around in a tank. Instead I want to talk about the people in my life you have known.

"You weren't surprised when Chuck disappeared?"
"He told me he was going to go."
"He told you!"
"I knew he was tired of running the business. He had built up his pet empire, but still he felt empty. He was tired of living in a comfortable, rich suburb in Cape Town, when there was a whole country and people out there he didn't know. Once he told me he didn't want to be sepa-

rated from them. It was the most extraordinary thing he ever said to me. Also, Chuck was disappointed with his sons. I think sometimes he was too hard on them. They certainly didn't understand him."

"My father almost never spoke about Chuck. It was like he couldn't bring himself to talk about his father. I never heard anything about him so I never asked questions. Oh, I heard all the stories about the rhinos and the Knysna elephants, but they always spoke of him as if he was a crazy eccentric."

"Your grandfather was going crazy at that time. I knew he felt he'd reached an end of a life and was going to leave."

"Did you know what he was going to do? I mean, where was he going?"

"Jay, I don't have all the answers. You must remember I was very busy with my own research, and your grandfather was a hard man to understand. Besides, I don't think he knew himself. He kept on talking about the injustices of the system he lived under, how he despised the government. That's why everyone thought he had left the country. But I knew he could never do that. He loved the place too much to leave it. Besides, it wasn't in Chuck's nature to run away."

"But he did run away from his family and life in Cape Town," said Jay bitterly.

"That's true, but I never felt he would run away from South Africa."

"He didn't. I met some people yesterday in Khayelitsha who'd seen him fit and healthy only two years ago. Arthur Jacobs, a friend of his, had just died the day I arrived, but his widow told me she'd sent the box to someone called May Eventide, who lives somewhere in Mossel Bay. Have you ever heard of her?"

"No, I haven't. So, are you going to Mossel Bay?"

"I don't seem to have any choice. I really want to find

the box Gramps left me. Mrs. Jacobs was sure it had been delivered to a friend up the coast. The box was obviously important to Chuck."

"Have you thought to phone and find out if it's still there?"

"I was given an address, but I wasn't given a telephone number, and when I phoned enquiries they said there was no number listed under that address. No, the Ark is going to have to take me there. I hope she'll make it." He paused. "Tell me about Uncle Peter, Bob. When I told you what happened the day I went to Camps Bay, you didn't say very much. You've just said Chuck was disappointed in his sons. I don't understand how he could have been disappointed in Peter. He's the son who made it. He's successful and rich."

"Chuck wanted his two sons to take over the pet empire. Peter wasn't interested in animals and he moved into other fields. And so the whole burden of the business fell on your father's shoulders. He didn't cope very well with it, as you know."

Suddenly Bob Lo seemed to feel he had said enough. He stood up, went slowly over to the door, and opened it. Before he went into the hatchery he turned back to his assistant.

"Jay, I don't know about everything that happened in your family over the past few years, but I do know there was bad blood between your father and his half brother."

"I realized that. Uncle Peter seemed to think I knew something terrible about him, but I didn't know what he was talking about."

Bob Lo gazed at Jay for a moment.

"Sometimes it's better to leave the past alone and move into the future."

Sometimes it's better to shut up and return to water and rainbows and not get involved with the adult world. I feel I'm being drawn into a dark tunnel crammed wall-to-wall with ugly adults.

"Thanks, Bob. I appreciate you talking to me. I needed to hear that stuff about my grandfather. My mother doesn't talk much about the family, so I don't know anything about what makes the Watsons tick."

Jay followed Bob Lo into the hatchery and for the rest of the afternoon worked among the tanks and fishes. As he dipped his hand into the cool water he recalled what immersion had felt like. It was a long time since he had last submerged in the tanks, and he thought nostalgically of the pleasures of his fantasy world. His new commitment to tracking down the yellowwood box left little time for anything else.

If Bob Lo had not been in the room he would have stripped and returned to the water. The desire had come on again, as powerfully as ever before—the desire for the safe, watery womb, where King Khoi ruled in a tranquil world of rainbow mirages and the Princess Moonlight was graceful and beautiful—because, outside, the real world was dangerous and bewildering.

Straightening up from cleaning the last tank, he was startled to see Levi Bam standing in the doorway. The boy's face was smeared with blood, and he wiped his nose with a hand already sticky and red.

"Levi! What is it?" Jay asked, appalled and also surprised by the sudden appearance of the small boy.

"I want to go to the cemetery—to Leviticus," Levi answered in a strangled voice.

"Hang on, I'll fetch some tissues," said Bob Lo, and he quickly went into the office while Jay inspected Levi's face.

"Leave it! It doesn't matter. I want to go now!"

"Calm down, Lee, calm down. What's going on? What happened to your face?"

"I tripped," Levi said quickly, avoiding Jay's eyes. "I don't care about the blood. I just want to get back at him. I want to kill him."

"Who?"

"That man. Jenny's boyfriend."

Bob Lo came back with a bowl of water and some tissues. He tried to clean up the bleeding nose, but Levi jerked away from him. "Leave me alone. Take me to the cemetery, Jay."

"You'll tell me what happened?"

The boy nodded.

"You promise?"

"Yes."

The boy turned on his heel and walked out of the hatchery.

Bob Lo and Jay exchanged glances.

"You'd better do what he wants. He's in some sort of trouble. Poor little beggar," Bob Lo said, shaking his head. "Trouble follows him around like a shadow."

Levi and Jay ended up walking to the cemetery in silence. The boy refused to say what had happened, and Jay stopped trying to force it out of him. Levi was filled with a rage so intense that he was unable to speak. Every now and then he would wipe away a trickle of blood from his swollen nose with the tissues Bob Lo had given him. Glancing down at him, Jay saw that his upper lip was also swollen.

What happens to you in the war zone of your home, Lee? Is it a house filled with sharp corners and long falls? Or is there something else?

At the cemetery, Jay looked around to see if they were being observed and then bent open the wire where he had made the hole in the fence. Levi slipped through and went immediately to the bottom of the cemetery. Jay guessed what he was up to, and so, after squirming through the fence himself, he sat down to wait for Levi.

My morbid little friend, Levi Bam, communing with the spirit
of a dead boy whose middle name is Leviticus. Weird.

Levi was standing among the statues and gravestones, looking intently at the small statue of another boy from another time, and Jay thought he could see his lips moving.

After a while Jay walked over to Levi and sat down on the edge of a tombstone.

"Do you want to talk about it, old man?"

"One day I am going to kill Gary. I know I will."

"Don't you think that's a bit extreme?"

"I don't care, I know I will."

"Did he do that to you?" Jay asked, indicating Levi's face.

"It's nothing. I don't feel it anymore. He's not my father. I don't have to listen to him, or to my mother either. She didn't want me. She told me. She tried to get rid of me when I was in her, she told me that too. I don't belong here. I belong there." He pointed at the other boy. "If she'd done it, I wouldn't be here, but she was too late. That's what she said. She was too late. She never wanted me. I was a mistake."

The words came out in short, rapid-fire bursts, and by the time he had finished speaking he was breathless. Jay was speechless.

Levi fought to hold back the tears, bit his swollen top lip, and pointed again at the stone boy who looked steadily back at him.

"I belong there."

"Hey, old man, that's not true, your mother loves you."

"Loving is not enough."

Jay was silenced.

Slowly Levi withdrew his gaze from the statue. After a long while he sighed and began to walk toward the hole in the cemetery fence. They climbed through, and Jay bent the wire back into place.

"On Monday we go to Mossel Bay?"

"Yes, Levi, we leave early in the morning," Jay said, looking down into the pale, exhausted face of the boy.

"That's good."

THE ARK WAS ON ITS WAY again, humming past the stud farms of Somerset West, over Sir Lowry's Pass, past the small town of Caledon, and into the hills of the Overberg. Solidly it held the road, hugging the corners, speeding down the hills, and sailing up the steep gradients.

Jay felt there was nothing finer than driving with a sunroof down, your elbow out of an open window, and a tune running through your head. His eyes passed over the countryside flowing past him.

Ah, land so beautiful! Land so cruel!

Jay laughed out loud.

Getting a little poetical, Jay-o. And why not? It's a perfect day. The sun is bright and warm, the sky is clear, and the road is smooth.

"What were you laughing at?" asked Levi from beside him.

"Nothing, Lee, just nothing—and everything. So, you didn't have any trouble getting out this morning?"

"No problem," Levi said, not taking his eyes off the road.

Looking down at the small boy next to him, Jay was aware of his fragility. After they had left the cemetery on Saturday, Jay had bought Levi an ice-cream cone, and they had gone down to the station to watch trains. He had tried again to get the boy to tell him what had happened to him earlier that day, but Levi wouldn't say anything. Jay had assumed he was being loyal to his mother and had respected him for that, and so had changed the subject and talked about the forthcoming journey. Slowly Levi had returned to his usual somber self.

"No problem at all." Levi's voice had its normal measured quality. The boy did not seem able to express any degree of emotion other than blind rage.

Levi, the great leveler. Is there anything that will bring back a lost childhood, a lost boy? Especially one who is taking a drug to calm him down.

"We're coming up to Swellendam in another ten kilometers. We should check the water, Mr. Lottee," Andy called from the back of the van.

Andy and Lungile had approached their parents with the cunning of secret agents to ask them for permission to go with Jay. It was, after all, the holidays, Andy had reasoned with his father, who anyway was pleased his son was getting on so well with Margaret's son. He needed to get to know some white kids in the area, Lungile had pointed out to his father, who had been forced to agree.

"It's a good idea to stop for a while and give the engine a rest," said Mr. Lottee, slowing down as they approached the off-ramp to the old Overberg town of Swellendam.

The Ark drew up at a petrol station in Swellendam, and its passengers climbed out to buy cold drinks, check the tire pressure, and fill the van up with petrol. Then, after the short break, they were on the road again.

After they had left Swellendam the conversation turned to the subject of grandfathers. Jay had been telling them how he wished he had gotten to know his grandfather better.

"My grandfather," Lungile began, "was the first medical doctor in his village. He went to Johannesburg to study medicine at the University of Witwatersrand. In those days it was very difficult for black people to study: My grandfather was one of only five black students at the university. I know my grandfather well, because we all lived together in one house in Langa. When my father gets tough, I always turn to my grandfather, and he always takes my side."

"My grandfather was a policeman," Andy said. "Well, actually not a policeman, more like a detective. So we never saw him much, maybe on Christmas Day, and sometimes on my birthday. He was always busy on a case or tracking down a murderer. Like Jay, I never asked him any of the questions I wanted answers to. I heard all these weird things about him from other people, like how he was the bravest man on the force and was afraid of no one. He was given two medals after he died—which I thought was sort of dumb—and after that nobody really spoke much about him. Perhaps the way he died—"

"How did he die?" Jay asked.

"He shot himself."

Lungile whistled, and Andy fidgeted uneasily.

"I didn't find out about that until I was much older. By then he was just a photograph and somebody I thought of whenever I was sad. Like he was some kind of lost opportunity."

Exactly what I feel, Andy. A lost opportunity.

"I was always a little frightened of him. He was a big, strong man who didn't speak much and got angry quickly. Ja, but I think his life was more interesting than my father's. He's an insurance salesman."

"My grandfather wanted to kill me," Levi said, in the pause that followed Andy's last words.

"Levi, he did not!" Jay said.

"Yes, he did. I know. Before I was born he wanted my mother to have an absorption."

"You mean an abortion."

"Yes, that, and I know he wants me dead. I'm in the way. He called me an embarrassment and the ruin of Jenny's life. I was hiding under the table when he and Jenny were talking. No, they weren't talking, they were fighting. I don't ever want to get to know him. I hate him."

"What about your grandfather, Mr. Lottee?" Jay asked hastily, diverting attention from the boy who had suddenly reddened.

"My grandfather was the kindest, gentlest man I've ever met," said Mr. Lottee. "He told me that being short meant I was closer to the earth, and so able to listen more carefully to what it said to me. I'll never forget that. My parents took me over to Turkey to visit him. Before that we'd never met. I had only heard about him. When he saw me for the first time do you know what he said? 'There's a little gentleman who will change the world.' That's what he said. Change the world. I cried and cried when we had to go home. My mother promised we would go back to Turkey to see him again one day. We never did, and by the time I was old enough to go by myself he had died. I felt I knew my grandfather even though I'd only spent two months with him. But I understand what you said, Jay. I also would have liked to have spent longer with him, but the time I had was enough. That was the way it was meant to be."

They all fell silent after Mr. Lottee had finished speaking. Jay was thinking about an old man lying in bed, his head tilted at an awkward angle and his hands trying to write something on a piece of paper.

What were you trying to write, Gramps? I remember I tried to read it, but it was merely a squiggle. I think I still have it somewhere. And then you got so angry you broke the pencil. I wanted to cry for you then, but you saw the pity in my eyes and chased me out of the room.

"Hey, look, there's a hitchhiker," Lungile said. Mr. Lottee slowed down as the Ark approached the figure at the side of the road. Beside the hitchhiker was a small rucksack, and against the rucksack was a sign: "GOING ANYWHERE NORTH. PICK ME UP."

The hitchhiker was gazing out across the road at the countryside and the snatch of blue sea, which could be seen to the south, seemingly oblivious to the traffic streaming by. As the Ark drew nearer the figure turned casually in their direction and then looked back again at the view.

"Let's pick him up," Andy said. "We've got plenty of room in the back of the van."

"You know what they say about hitchhikers," Mr. Lottee warned.

"But he's all alone. Come on, what do you say, guys?"

"I don't mind," Jay said.

"Nor do I," Lungile agreed.

"Let's pick her up," said Levi.

Mr. Lottee slowed to a stop, and they saw Levi had been right. The hitchhiker was a young woman.

"Just my luck to get the slowest jalopy on the road," she said, as Jay leaned out of the window.

Mr. Lottee laughed, and the others looked at her nonplussed.

"Well, we don't need to give you a lift if you'd prefer to wait for a Porsche," said Andy, stung by the girl's comment about the van.

"We're going as far as Mossel Bay. If you want to come with us, there's plenty of room for you," Jay said.

"I get carsick, so I have to sit in the front. Okay?"

In stunned silence Jay got out of the van. He waited for the girl to climb into the front seat beside Levi, and then he got into the back of the van with the others.

"Thanks, that's sweet of you," she said, flinging a quick flick of a smile at him over her shoulder. She looked down at Levi, who grinned up at her. "Hello, kid, what's your name?"

"Levi."

"I'm going to call you Levi the Terrible. You've got a strange glint in your eye, and your nose is all askew. Okay?"

"Okay."

"I'm Mr. Lottee," Mr. Lottee said as he pulled away from the side of the road and changed gear.

"Hi. I'm Carol. Boy, this is neat. What do you keep in all those cages?"

"Supplies and stuff. This is the Ark and we're on a journey," Levi answered eagerly.

Levi, you are positively beaming. What's come over you, old man? I've never seen you so alive before. Look at that grinning kid! He can't keep his eyes off her.

Carol had cropped brown hair, freckles, deep-set, almond-shaped eyes, and a tiny plastic skull with green eyes dangling from one of her earlobes. In the other ear there was a row of earrings from the top of the ear down to the lobe. She wore denim pants with holes in both knees and a denim jacket with the American Confederate flag on its back. Her dirty feet were in leather sandals, and she wore several bangles on one arm. There were numerous rings on her fingers

"I'm Lungile."

"And I'm Andy, and this is—"

"And I'm not going to remember all your names, okay? With short rides like this I don't waste my time with getting all the names down. You know mine and that's fine, and I know Levi the Terrible and Mr. Lottee the driver. Good enough, don't you think?" Carol said, addressing Levi, who nodded vigorously and grinned back at her.

Andy, Lungile, and Jay rolled their eyes at one another.

"Where are you from?" Jay asked.

"Okay, here it comes! Listen carefully because I'm going to answer all small-talk questions in one go. I was born in Elsies River in 1973, and I don't know anyone who comes from there anymore. My father worked on the railways until he was laid off. My mother is a nurse. I have a fat-cat brother who works in the city in a suit. I'm going up to the

Transkei for a party. I don't do anything but travel. Sometimes I make jewelry and leather sandals, which I sell if I need some money. My hobbies are surfing, hanging out on the beach, and rock concerts. I don't have a boyfriend. I don't like the government, the ANC, or Inkatha, and I think the politics of South Africa suck."

Carol paused for breath, and then, before anyone could think of anything to say, she continued. "Ja, I think that about covers it all. Oh yes, one more thing: I don't do drugs, but I do do Lion Lager. Now, I've been on the road since five o'clock this morning so I'm going to sleep for a while. If you can hold off the questions for a bit, I'd really appreciate it. Okay, guys?"

Carol pulled out a Walkman, turned it on, and settled the earphones around her head. She arranged her rucksack against the van door, put her feet up on the dashboard, snuggled into her corner, and shut her eyes.

The group was silent for a while, apparently transfixed by the new passenger.

"Do you think we can talk?" Andy whispered.

"I don't think she's going to hear anything with those earphones on," Jay replied in a normal voice.

"What makes you think she's done a lot of hitchhiking?" Lungile asked wryly. They exchanged grins with one another.

"I told you we shouldn't pick up a hitchhiker," Mr. Lottee said, looking with distaste at the sleeping Carol.

"I think she's great," Levi said.

"You're just in love, old man."

"Hey, you guys, will you look at Lee! He's blushing," Andy said.

"Now that's a first. The only other time I've seen him go red is when he's angry," Jay said.

Levi folded his arms tightly and stared straight ahead, ignoring the laughter. His expression, however, was not quite as grim as usual. Despite himself, Mr. Lottee chuckled.

Carol slept soundly through the lunch stop and a flat tire that took them an hour to fix because they couldn't find the wrench. When she eventually woke up they were on the road again. It was late afternoon, and Jay, Lungile, and Andy were half asleep in the back of the van. The faint smell of petrol fumes, the blazing sun, and the constant motion had made them drowsy.

She woke to find the dark eyes of Levi staring at her.

"What are you looking at, Levi the Terrible?"

"Your earring. It's a skull, isn't it?"

"Oh, this piece of junk," Carol said, as she sat up, stretched her legs, and put her rucksack down by her feet. "My last boyfriend gave it to me. Romantic, huh?"

She yawned, an open-mouthed, stretching-catlike yawn.

"Why did he give you death?" Levi asked softly.

Carol sat up, shocked, and stared down at the small boy, who looked earnestly back at her. Her face softened.

"Where did you get to be so clever, Levi?"

"I saw it on the TV. Skull and crossbones means death."

"It's the kind of present drummers in heavy metal bands give a girl," Carol said, idly twisting the earring between her fingers. "I should throw it away, but I can't. It's something to remind me of that bastard." Her voice was flat and bitter.

"He didn't have to give you anything at all."

"I wish he hadn't, Levi. More than anything in the world I wish he hadn't. Hey, Levi, come here. I need a hug."

Carol put her arm around Levi and hugged him. The boy warmed to her touch and allowed himself to be held for a moment.

"How are you doing, Mr. Lottee?" Jay said, raising his voice above the noise of the engine.

"Just fine. I think we've got another couple of hours to go. Because of our late start this morning we might not get to Mossel Bay until after it's dark, Jay.'

"Blame it on me, guys. I should have done a better job

103

of tying up that exhaust pipe," Andy said, waking up and stretching.

"You're forgiven, Andy. But only this once. Mr. Lottee, the address is not really in Mossel Bay, more like somewhere close by."

"Where are you going?" Carol asked.

"To a place called Smokey Hill."

"Never heard of it."

"We'll find it," Mr. Lottee said.

Jay pulled out the scrap of paper Mrs. Jacobs had given him and read the address again: May Eventide, Smokey Hill, Mossel Bay.

"So why's it called the Ark?" asked Carol, turning around in the front seat to face those at the back, where Lungile was also waking up. She lit a cigarette and threw the match out the window.

"I named it. The van used to have all sorts of animals living in it," Levi said proudly.

"And now it's only got one animal—Levi the Terrible!" Carol said, tickling Levi, who squirmed and giggled at her touch.

"My grandfather was a traveling pet salesman . . ." Jay began.

"What do you mean?"

"He sold pets."

"Door to door?" Carol burst out laughing. "Madam, here is a fine example of a budgie who's been right around the world," she said in a funny accent. "And this parrot's been to Brakpan and back."

She laughed again, an uninhibited, raucous laugh, and Levi giggled with her. Jay tugged at his hair and pushed the strands away from his forehead.

She thinks she's funny. Even Lee's amused by her. A traveling comedian.

"Now, don't get huffy. I think your grandfather had a lot

of imagination. I mean the whole idea is brilliant! Who could resist buying from someone who carried his animals around with him? It is funny, not stupid funny, just fun funny."

"This was the van that started the Watson Pet Emporium business. You've heard of the chain of pet shops?"

"No, I haven't, but I'm sure they are magnificent."

I'm feeling stupid! Why do I have to defend my grandfather? Relax, Jay-o.

"So, tell me why you're going to Mossel Bay, and then I'll mind my own business."

And so the story was told again: how Chuck Watson turned up at Gordon Road after his stroke, Bob Lo's relationship with Chuck, Jay's meeting with his Uncle Peter after ten years, the journey into Khayelitsha to meet Arthur Jacobs. Carol was a good listener, and Jay found the story coming easily from him. He spoke fluently. He was no longer embarrassed by the nature of his quest, but spoke sincerely about his mixed feelings toward his grandfather.

"The yellowwood box could be empty for all I care, but at least I'm looking for it," Jay said.

"That's not true, Jay. You do care," Levi said.

"Actually, he hopes it's filled with gold nuggets," Lungile put in.

"No, I don't." Jay laughed.

"Well, I do!" said Andy.

"Don't forget the part about Lucky the horse," Levi interjected, and Jay picked up that detail and wound it into the narrative.

"Do you think maybe your grandfather left you some money? Perhaps the box has money in it," Carol said, intrigued by the mystery of the yellowwood box.

"No, I don't think so. He wasn't very rich when he died. My mother had to take him in because he couldn't afford to go to a clinic."

"It's a strange sort of thing to leave anyone in your will. A yellowwood box can't be worth very much," she said, shrugging her shoulders.

"It's very important," Levi said emphatically.

With that, the conversation came to an end, and they all fell silent, turning to watch dusk settling over the countryside.

The searching is sometimes more important than the finding. Get deep, Jay-o! Deep Inner Meaning, spells DIM. Maybe there isn't anything in it at all, and that will be fine too. Maybe.

Mr. Lottee switched on the headlights, and their beams spotlighted a road sign at the side of the highway. Jay had been staring idly out at the rapidly darkening countryside, but the sign caught his attention because it flashed "GH–MK 230 kilometers" as it streaked past. Or that was what Jay thought he saw, but before he could be sure the sign was gone.

"Did anyone see what that sign said?"

"What sign?" Lungile asked.

"I saw it, but I didn't read it," Mr. Lottee said. "What did it say?"

"I don't know—I thought I recognized something on it . . ."

GH–MK two hundred and thirty kilometers. Hmmmm?

"But I can't be sure," Jay said, staring out at the road to catch the next sign.

"Listen, guys, you can drop me off on the other side of Mossel Bay. Smokey Hill is on the other side, right? So you can drop me off there."

"Why don't you come with us?" Levi spoke up, stricken at the thought of losing his new friend so quickly.

"In another ten minutes it will be dark, Carol," Mr. Lottee added. "Do you think it's safe to hitchhike at night?"

"Well, it's true, not many people stop after dark," she said.

"I didn't think it would take us this long," Jay said.

"The van is old, and I didn't want to push her over seventy kilometers an hour," said Mr. Lottee defensively.

"We're going to have to phone your mother, Levi, and tell her that you'll be coming back tomorrow. We'll say the van broke down or something."

"She won't be back from the beach yet."

"Well, we must get hold of her sometime. Carol, if you like you can stay with us, and we'll drop you off tomorrow morning. We've got plenty of blankets and stuff."

"Okay, I'm in no hurry. The Transkei's not going anywhere. Now I can get to know this little terror a bit better," she said, nudging Levi, who beamed at her and nudged her back.

Levi, I've never seen you so happy! Where did that gloomy old man with the faraway look in his eyes go? Carol, you're pushing all the right buttons. Keep on pushing them.

The Ark reached Mossel Bay at eight o'clock. They arrived just in time still to see the blue spread of the sea open out in front of them as the road dipped down to the coast. Carol insisted that they stop. Mr. Lottee pulled over to the side of the road, and they climbed out and sat on the roof, watching the sea turn to satin as evening fell.

"Traveling doesn't mean you'll automatically see stuff. You must stop so you can notice the small things," Carol said, leaning against the hood as the boys tried to take in what it was she was seeing.

"Like me," Levi added, sitting on the bumper, staring out at the changing colors of the water.

When it was dark they drove into Mossel Bay and asked for directions to Smokey Hill. After taking several wrong turns they eventually found a road that they thought might lead them to May Eventide's house.

As the van climbed the gentle slope of Smokey Hill, lights began to appear in the countryside below them. The Ark bumped along a dusty track for twenty minutes before the headlights fell on a metal sign that read "Eventide."

"Is this woman expecting you?" Carol asked as Lungile opened the gate into the property.

"I don't know. No, I don't think so."

From the gate they could see a dim light glowing at the top of the hill. As the Ark made its way up a rough dirt track toward the light they heard the sound of children singing.

THE DIRT TRACK led to four buildings standing around a circular driveway. A Jeep was parked in the clearing. The buildings were dark except for the largest one, from which the singing came. The travelers got out of the Ark and looked around.

A small figure appeared silhouetted in the doorway of the building. "Tannie, there's people here!" a young voice called over the sound of the singing.

The singing stopped. The doorway and windows quickly filled up with what appeared to be young children staring out at the van.

"Do you think this is the right place?" Mr. Lottee whispered to Jay.

"It did say Eventide on the sign."

A woman carrying a small child pushed her way through the crowd in the doorway and walked over to the group by the van. What seemed to be about thirty black children, very suspicious of the strangers standing in the darkness, hesitantly followed her.

The woman, in her late fifties, was tall, with straw-colored hair fastened on top of her head. Her full skirt and checked man's shirt, rolled up at the sleeves, hung loosely on her wiry figure. The child in her arms eyed Jay and his friends and grinned, while the other children huddled for safety behind her. Jay stepped forward to greet her.

My grandfather knew this woman. This is May Eventide.

"You must be Jason Watson. I'm May Eventide," said the woman, smiling at Jay but looking past him at the van. She laughed at his look of surprise. "Chuck would have hated the color you painted his van. How does the old devil run? Is she still breathing fire and smoke? And is the clutch still giving you problems?"

She laughed again as the group groaned. She spoke briefly in Xhosa to the child in her arms. He shook his head and laid it on her shoulder.

"Ja, I had a problem with the clutch," Andy said, immediately warming to the woman, who seemed to know the van's idiosyncracies as well as he did. "I had to put in a new clutch plate, and now it's as good as ever."

"I told Chuck he really should replace some parts every now and then, but he never listened. I'm glad she's got you to take care of her, young man. What's your name?"

"I'm Andy le Roux."

"Andy, I'm very pleased to meet the man responsible for rejuvenating the old devil. You've done an excellent job. I didn't even hear you coming up the hill. I used to hear Chuck coming for miles."

Andy glowed at her appreciation of his efforts.

"This is Mr. Lottee, Lungile Masakela, Levi Bam, and Carol," said Jay. Everyone shook hands formally with the tall woman, addressing her as Mrs. Eventide. She told them to call her by her Christian name, and then turned back to Jay.

"It's good to see Chuck's van again, but even better to meet you at last, Jason. I've heard so much about you."

"You have?"

"Of course! Chuck was very proud of you. He always told me that you had great potential—and the reddest hair he'd ever seen. 'He's a very special child,' he would say. I never doubted it, and here you are with the Ark—I like the name, Chuck would have liked it too—coming to see me with your friends, just as I knew you would."

"You knew I was coming?"

"No, I didn't know for certain, but I suspected that you

110

might, someday. I'm just surprised it took you so long. Why, it's six months since Chuck died, isn't it?"

Jay nodded.

"Was it bad?" she asked gently.

Unexpectedly, Jay's eyes brimmed with tears, and he choked as he tried to answer the question. May Eventide had done more than surprise him with her obvious intimacy with his grandfather. She had also succeeded in calling up a sense of Chuck Watson's presence all around them.

Gramps, you were here, alive, whole, walking around this place. I can feel you around me. Tears—where from? This is stupid. I can't speak.

"I'm sorry, I'm just feeling funny at the moment," Jay gulped, mortified by his sudden display of emotion.

"It doesn't matter. Don't worry, Jason. We'll talk later. We were just singing our goodnight blessing. Join us while we finish, and then I'll make some tea. You all look a little road weary."

Turning to the children, who had been intently examining the strangers, May said, "Come on, everyone, we're going to sing to some friends. This is Chuck's grandson."

The older children crowded around Jay, reaching out to grasp his hand. Some repeated Chuck's name and asked various questions about him. Three little girls quickly took charge of Carol and Levi, and other children took Mr. Lottee, Lungile, and Andy by their hands and pulled them toward the building where the dim light shone. They moved in an excited bustle out of the clearing and into a big room that was evidently used as a dormitory.

The room had a row of triple-decker wooden bunk beds running down the length of each of its longest walls. Small ladders went up the bunks, and on each bed there was a blanket and a pillow. In the corners of the room, upon triangular wooden shelves, paraffin lamps flickered, casting

111

ghostly shadows on the ceiling. In the center stood a long table with two benches tucked underneath it. The furniture was rough but practical and looked handmade.

I sit in a fish tank and dream of rainbows and fantastic lands with tropical fish princesses and goldfish kings. I sit in a fish tank and complain about life.

The children stood around the table and looked at May, waiting for her signal.

"Tonight is a special night. We have visitors from Chuck's family. Some of you remember Chuck . . ."

Shouts of pleasure greeted May's words, and several of the children started to chant. "Chuck-a-luck, Chuck the man, catch you, fast as anyone can! Chuck-a-luck, Chuck-a-luck, Chuck-a-luck!"

"As you can hear," said May, obviously enjoying the puzzled expression on Jay's face, "some of my children have long memories. He was very important to them. But I can see you knew nothing about all this, Jason."

"Not a thing!"

"Chuck, you old reprobate! You didn't even tell your own grandson about our dream for Eventide!" May exclaimed.

Jay swung around, half expecting to find his grandfather standing behind them.

"We've got a great deal to talk about, Jason. But first let's say goodnight to the children."

May Eventide spoke to the children in Xhosa. One of the older boys started the singing in flawless tones of a voice not yet broken, and after a while the dense rough-and-tumble harmonies of the other children joined in. The travelers from the Ark listened as the group of children filled the room with exuberant song and rejoiced in what united them with the world. They sang a Xhosa praise song, an Afrikaans psalm, and, last, an English hymn, which Jay and his friends sang with them when they recognized the tune.

Jay glanced over at May. She had forgotten her visitors for the moment. She was watching her children and singing along with them. In the flickering lamplight her lined and worn face was beautiful. She was still holding the small child, and he nestled into her shoulder.

When they had finished singing May laid the child down on the nearest cot. She moved around among some of the smaller children and started putting them to bed. Carol, who had been standing in the doorway, came into the room, gathered up some of the others, and lifted them up into their bunks. Levi walked beside her, smiling at the children as Carol tucked in the blankets around them.

"This is amazing," Andy whispered to Jay, noting the orderly manner in which the children prepared for bed.

"Come on, you three, come and help," Carol called from the end of the room. The children picked up her suggestion, and several small boys tugged Jay, Andy, and Lungile forward, clutching their hands and guiding them to the bunks. Mr. Lottee, unaccustomed to dealing with children, remained standing by the door until one of the girls realized he had escaped their attention and captured him. The room was filled with excited chatter as the youngsters organized their visitors. Lungile spoke Xhosa to some of his charges, and Andy lifted his giggling guide up on his shoulders and threw him onto a top bunk. One little boy, about the same age as Levi, patiently waited by his bunk until Jay could reach him to tuck him in. The boy was small, delicately boned, with opaque round, dark eyes. Jay lifted him and placed him on his bunk.

"What's your name?"

"Nelson."

"That's a good name to have."

"I've named myself after Nelson Mandela. May said I could."

"That's great," Jay said and tucked him in.

"Will you be here tomorrow?" Nelson asked, lying with his arms folded across his chest and looking earnestly up at Jay.

"I think so."

"Good. I'll see you in the morning."

Soon all the children were in bed. May put out all but one of the paraffin lamps and told everyone to leave.

"Not you Jason. I want to show you something."

The others went out into the cool night air, leaving Jay alone with May in the dormitory.

She led Jay to an open window at the back of the room. As they passed through the length of the dormitory all eyes followed them. On the window ledge there was a cup of water, some bread, some fruit, and a book.

"This is for Chuck. All of the other boys think of Chuck as their grandfather, and when I told them that he'd died and wouldn't be coming back here anymore, they wanted to do this for him. Do you know what it means?"

"No," Jay answered, picking up the book. It was a collection of Greek myths retold for children.

"In some African cultures when a person dies he doesn't ever go away, but stays around to watch over his family. He becomes an ancestor spirit, and if his family remembers him he brings them good fortune."

"These kids think of my grandfather as a ghost?"

Surrender to the powers of the moon card and the underworld goddess Hecate and her three-headed dog, Uncle Peter Pumpkin Eater said.

"Not a ghost, but a benevolent shade. That family members should be remembered is the important part. Sometimes if they are forgotten they will not stay close to protect the family. That's why the boys have done this," May said, indicating the windowsill.

Uncle Peter said to give myself over to the powers of the moon. That something I felt trying to get through to me, that sense of waiting, as if I were being spoken to. A sense of someone being around me . . .

"I thought you'd like to see a little of what Chuck meant to the boys, and how they remember him." Then, seeing the bewilderment on Jay's face, May said, "I'm sorry. This has all been a little too much for you. I should have waited."

"No, it's not that. I can't explain it, May, but ever since I've started on this journey, I've been having strange thoughts, and what you've just said triggered off some more of them."

"We'll talk later. Now let me say my goodnight to the children. I'll join you outside," May said.

Jay went outside to join the others, who were standing in the clearing beside the Ark. Behind them, out across the valley, just above the horizon, hung a large silver globe. With a jolt Jay realized it was the full moon, floating detached and beautiful in the night sky.

Rising moon, in the sky
are you watching over I?

"Wasn't that singing something else? Incredible!" Carol said, voicing everyone's thoughts as they turned toward Jay.

"You didn't tell us we were coming to some sort of an orphanage," said Lungile, and then asked anxiously, as he caught sight of Jay's face, "Jay, are you all right?"

"Look!" Jay pointed to the rising moon behind them.

"Wow!" Andy said.

They moved to the other side of the Ark to see the moon better.

"Isn't it beautiful?" Carol said, crouching down and hugging her knees.

"It's the moon. It's meant to be beautiful," Levi said solemnly. Then for several moments they were all quiet.

"Did you know your grandfather spent so much time here?" Mr. Lottee asked, breaking the silence.

"No, I didn't. I remember him talking about some boys or other, but I couldn't always understand what he said. The stroke had affected his speech, and he wasn't always in the best of moods. He never told me about this place."

"I want to come and live here and be one of May's children," Levi said.

"Now don't get any ideas into your head, old man."

"What a remarkable woman," Mr. Lottee said, gazing back at the dormitory. "She seems to run this place by herself."

May Eventide walked out of the dormitory and came over to where the group was standing.

"I think they're so excited about your visit it will be some time before they'll go to sleep, so I've left one lamp burning. Thank you very much, everybody. It's so good for the children to have visitors."

"I was speaking to Nelson—"

"Nelson has AIDS," May interrupted Jay. "He was born with the virus. The doctors have given him two, maybe three more years. He's one of my special children."

"That little boy, in the first bed?" Carol asked in disbelief. "But he looks so healthy."

"Winters are the worst time. If he gets a bad cold it will kill him," said May, and then, aware of the dampener she had cast on the group, she changed the subject. "Come inside, I'll make some tea. We're a little low on milk and sugar, but I think I can scrape something together."

May's house had three rooms. The low front door opened into the middle room and was crammed with a couch, a desk littered with papers, a chair, a large beanbag in the corner, shelves of books, and a refrigerator.

"There's not much space, so sit wherever you can." She said a few words to Lungile in Xhosa, and he followed her into the next room, returning with two more chairs. "Here you are, Mr. Lottee and Carol."

"Levi and I are fine over here," Carol said, as she and the boy flopped down onto the beanbag.

On the walls were wool tapestries, an Indian carpet, and a pin board with photographs. A blue-and-white China tea set sat high up on a top shelf. Every available space in the room was in use. There was a guitar in one corner and a pile of newspapers, exercise books, papers, and a stack of phone directories in another.

No sign of your yellowwood box, Gramps.   ·

From where Jay sat he could see into the room from which Lungile had fetched the extra chairs. That room held a double bed covered with a crocheted bedspread, a heavy wooden wardrobe—the largest piece of furniture in the room—and a dressing table with a mirror. Everything in May Eventide's home was functional and well worn.

May busied herself making tea in the third room. This was smaller than the first two and doubled as a kitchen and a dining room. A metal table stood in the center of the room, and a sink and a stove took up much of the rest of the space.

"I haven't had so many visitors in a long time. I hope you are going to stay for a while?" May called from the kitchen.

"We haven't made any definite plans, but we thought we would go back to Cape Town tonight."

"Oh, you can't do that! Not after coming so far. We've a lot to talk about, Jason. You must spend the night here. I know there isn't much space, but we can find room."

"Well, I don't know, we don't want to put—"

"I'm staying," Levi said emphatically.

"I think I'd better phone your mother first, Levi."

"No, you don't have to. I'm staying," Levi repeated.

"Doesn't look like anything you say is going to make the terror change his mind," said Carol, amused at the irritated look on Jay's face.

Great, I get to deal with one of Lee's temper tantrums.

"How do you feel, Mr. Lottee?"

"I wouldn't like to drive back now. My eyes aren't so good at night. It looks like we'll have to sleep somewhere."

"I'd like to spend the night here and see some more of the kids tomorrow," Lungile said.

"Me too," Andy interjected.

"I'm just the hitchhiker, I don't mind what you do," Carol said, as the boys looked for her reaction. "I think this place is pretty cool. Whatever you do will suit me."

"I'll have to phone Jenny—Levi, don't look at me like that. Give me the telephone number and I'll phone your mother. May, where's the nearest phone?"

"In the bedroom, Jason."

"Oh? But I tried—I thought you didn't have a phone."

"Yes, I do, but it's an unlisted number."

Reluctantly Levi gave Jenny's number. Jay dialed several times, but no one answered at the other end.

"I told you—they haven't come home from their sailing yet," Levi said smugly.

"Well, there's nothing I can do about it at the moment, but Levi, don't forget to take your medicine."

"Well then, that's settled. You're all staying the night. I'll organize your beds later, but in the meantime here's the tea I promised you. Have you eaten yet?" May asked.

"Yes, we had something earlier," lied Jay, glaring at Andy, who was about to answer differently.

"Now, Jason, there really is enough to eat. As basic as things look here, we do have enough food for everyone. It's not going to be a three-course meal, but I have some soup and bread left over from the main meal. Who would like something to eat?"

"I'm starving!" Levi said desperately, and everyone laughed.

"Come on, bring your tea into the kitchen and help me get some supper together."

Everybody moved into the kitchen. Carol and Levi sliced and buttered bread. Andy and Lungile washed plates and spoons, while May took a pot of soup from the refrigerator and heated it up. Jay and Mr. Lottee sat at the table, as Jay once again recounted what had brought him to Eventide.

"Do you know, Jason," mused May, "at none of the times Chuck stayed with us did he ever tell me what was in that precious box. I was curious, but whenever I asked about it, he always avoided answering me directly. I knew it was very important to him, because he always had it with him, but I never saw him open it. When he was here for long periods, he would put it under the bed and there it would stay, until he got another bee in his bonnet and was off on his travels again."

"So he didn't stay here all the time?"

"Chuck Watson stay in one place for any length of time?" May seemed amused at the idea. "That will be the day! I used to see another bout of wanderlust coming long before even he recognized it. He would start rising earlier and earlier in the mornings and go for long walks before breakfast. Then he would get irritable, and we'd shout at each other over the stupidest things. Eventually he'd be unbearable and I would literally chase him off Eventide. He would start up the old van and roar out of here in a huff. I remember once when he was particularly fed up, the old devil wouldn't start. There he sat behind the wheel, cursing and shouting, fighting a van that wasn't going anywhere." She laughed happily at the memory. "He would always return after a month or two, subdued, apologetic, bearing gifts, and missing Eventide."

"Where would he go?"

"He spent a lot of time with Klasie up at Phantom Pass in the Knysna forest. Sometimes he would disappear into the karoo for a while. Once he went all the way up to Swakopmund; he spent quite a long time there. He also went several times to the Transkei, and Swaziland and the northern Transvaal."

"But what was he doing?"

"Just traveling. Seeing this wonderful, terrible land, he would say when he was in a poetic mood. Chuck wanted to see everything in South Africa. He said that too many people either had their heads in the sand or were living in some European fantasy; not enough people were living here, in this country, this South Africa—Africa, not Europe, not America. He used to get very worked up about the political situation. He was passionate about most things. In fact, that was the great thing about Chuck. 'Passion, May, Passion with a capital P, that's what makes life worth living,' he'd roar at me. I would laugh at him and tell him he was too old for passion, but he had his moments."

"Older men always make better lovers," Carol said solemnly, and the boys burst out laughing.

"That's not what I meant, Carol," May said, smiling and blushing slightly. "Anyway, enough of this reminiscing, we're boring your friends, Jason. You and I will talk later. The soup's ready. Andy and Lungile, have you finished the dishes?"

The soup was divided up, and everyone ate heartily. The conversation was lively and full of questions about Eventide. May told them how she had started the orphanage and school for children who were abandoned by their parents.

"I've been running Eventide on a wing and a prayer for

seven years now. That's when your grandfather helped me get this place started, Jason. When he heard about my idea, he gave me a great deal of money, and I was able to buy this land and the old buildings. The dormitory used to be a cowshed, and this building used to be a dairy. When you go into the dormitory tomorrow take another look at those bunks. Chuck made every single one of them. Every time there was no bed for a new child, he would set about making another triple bunk. Nowadays I run this place on donations from all sorts of people; sometimes I even have to go from house to house in the neighborhood asking for spare clothes, blankets, and books. Your grandfather put a lot of money into this place, and now that he's gone it's going to be hard to find another donor as generous as he was."

So that's what you did with the money you took with you. That's why you came back penniless. That's why you were so angry to find my father running the business into the ground. You were too busy being the good Samaritan elsewhere. You had found another family, a family you thought was more grateful and needy than your own.

May asked Jay questions about many people she knew only by name, and Jay told her about his grandmother, who swallowed spoons, his mother, Uncle Peter, and Chuck's friend, Bob Lo. The rest of the group ate in silence, except when they inserted their own stories as Jay came to the part where each of them had become involved with him.

"I've just remembered. I've got something special for tonight," Carol cried suddenly. jumping up from the table and leaving the room.

When the others had finished eating, Andy and Lungile cleared the table and washed the dishes. May got up and lit two candles, which shed placed in the center of the table. "I try to keep the electricity bill down, so in the evenings I use candles."

121

Levi left the room to find Carol, and the others busied themselves tidying the kitchen. In the soft light of the candles the room was cozy and warm. May sat down near Jay, who was quietly looking around the kitchen for some glimpse of what he had come for. There was no sign of the yellowwood box. In a low voice, so that no one else in the room could hear, May said, "You're looking for more traces of Chuck, Jay?"

Jay flushed.

"Look on the bookshelf above the stove. All those books belonged to Chuck."

Jason got up and pulled out one of the books. It was *Gods, Heroes and Men of Ancient Greece.* He pulled out another book, *The Greek Myths* by Robert Graves. He glanced over the titles of the six other books on the shelf: They all had something to do with Greek mythology and the stories of ancient Greece. The title *Jason and the Golden Fleece* caught his eye. Jay pulled out the brightly covered book and flicked through the well-worn pages.

"Ah, you've found Chuck's favorite story, Jason. Do you know it?"

"Not all that well," he replied, opening the book to the first page.

"Chuck was fascinated by Greek literature," said May. "He knew all the stories of Oedipus, the trials of Heracles, and the travels of Odysseus. Whenever he wasn't working on Eventide he would take out one of his books and read. Nothing could distract him once he'd begun. He said they were the first stories man had ever told, and that all other stories came from them. He would often read them aloud to the children. One of their favorite books is on the window ledge in the dormitory. But read that one, Jason, it won't take you long." Then, turning to Andy, Lungile, and Mr. Lottee, May invited them into the next room to show them photographs of the building of Eventide.

How many times did you turn these pages and read this story to your boys and girls, Gramps?

Jay fingered the slightly worn top corner of the first page and started to read:

> Jason grew up in a dark cave, high up in the mountains overlooking the Greek city Iolkos. He lived with an old man, a Centaur, who looked after him as if he were his own son. One day Centaur Chiron told Jason why he had been forced to grow up in the cave, and what the young prince had to do to reclaim what rightfully belonged to him . . .

Jay read how the young man left the cave, confronted his uncle Pelias, and demanded rule of the kingdom according to his right; how Pelias was frightened, for an oracle had warned him of a man wearing one sandal; and how Jason had arrived with only one foot shod, having lost the other sandal while helping an old lady cross a river. Jay read how Pelias promised the young prince he would comply with his demand if Jason would go to Colchis on the Black Sea and bring back the Golden Fleece.

So Jason proceeded to build a ship with fifty oars, the *Argo,* and gathered together the most famous heroes of Greece to set forth in search of the fabled Golden Fleece. Their voyage was full of incident: They had to struggle against men, the elements, and monsters.

After many trials—and here Jay paused to look at the picture of ferocious soldiers springing from the teeth of a dragon to stop the hero from escaping—Jason returned to Iolkos with the Golden Fleece. There he discovered his father had been put to death by Pelias when Jason was an infant His uncle was certain Jason would never return from the dangerous journey. Jason avenged himself on his uncle and reigned as king of Iolkos.

Jay closed the book and looked at its cover.

I can hear you reading this aloud, Gramps. How the children must have loved you. Jason and the Golden Fleece. Interesting.

"Chuck liked that story best of all, because it had a hero who had to rely on more than just his brains and physical strength." May was leaning against the doorway, looking at Jay. "Jason had to rely on his creative imagination to get what he wanted. He had to trust its power, even when he couldn't understand it. Chuck identified with that idea, and tried to teach it to the Eventide children."

Jay replaced the book on the shelf and came back to the table.

"You knew Chuck for seven years?"

"Yes, and I know what you're thinking. The answer to that question is also yes."

"I just wondered . . ."

"Of course you did. I would have done so too."

"But you knew he was married and had just disappeared without telling anyone where he was going?"

"Not at first, Jason. I didn't know that at first. He lied to me in the beginning."

May spoke quietly, reliving the time when a lie had caused pain and tears, and had endangered a friendship.

"When I found out the truth we had our most serious fight. We fought bitterly, and I resolved to have nothing more to do with Chuck Watson. He acknowledged that he had been wrong to mislead me, but he refused to leave it at that. He was very persistent, and as I found out more about him I began to understand why he had behaved as he had. Remember, Jason, I met him three years after he'd left his family. Now I know it may sound as if I'm making excuses, but as time went by, I began to love him. In the end I came to terms with his past. He was a special man and I didn't want to lose him."

Your honesty is astonishing, May Eventide. How must it have affected that old fraud, Chuck? I'm sure he didn't want to lose you either.

"An evening like this deserves a celebration!" cried Carol, bursting into the room with a bottle in her hand. "I always carry around a bottle of sherry for these occasions."

Carol put the sherry on the table and May got up to get glasses for everyone.

"I want to propose a toast," Carol announced, once the sherry had been poured. "To the Ark and her enterprise. If she hadn't stopped for me I wouldn't be here to meet you, May, and your children and Levi the Terrible. To the journey of the Ark!"

"The journey of the Ark!" chorused everyone, and they all drank.

"It tastes like cough mixture," Levi said.

"It's supposed to taste like that, Levi," said Carol, putting an arm around the boy and drawing him to her. "Here, I'll drink yours if you don't want it."

"No way!" Levi responded, keeping his glass out of Carol's reach.

"I'd like to propose a toast to Jason, for following the pull of his heart and bringing you all to Eventide," May said, raising her glass.

"To Jason!"

After more sharing of stories, and more questions answered, the evening began to wind down. Levi fell asleep in Carol's lap, and this prompted May to collect spare blankets and prepare beds for everyone. Andy and Lungile said they would sleep in the Ark, and, taking pillows and blankets, they said goodnight to the others. Mr. Lottee and Jay were given spare beds in the dormitory, and Mr. Lottee said goodnight, too, and disappeared.

"Come, little one, time for everyone to sleep," Carol said

softly to Levi, sound asleep in her arms. She carried him to the beanbag and lay down next to him, wrapping her arms around his slight body.

Levi slept with his mouth open. The small, angular face no longer looked tight and strained. He slept in a strangely twisted fashion, head turned to one side, body wrapped around toward Carol. May laid a blanket over them very gently, but Levi woke up immediately. One arm came up abruptly to his chest, and the other wrapped itself protectively across his face.

"Shh, Levi, it's only May. Here's a blanket."

Levi stared wide-eyed at May for a moment, checked for Carol—"I'm here, Levi"—and then dropped back to sleep.

Nightmares catching you so soon into sleep, old man?

"Come, Jason," May whispered. She blew out the candles in the kitchen and led the way outside. They sat down on a bench at the side of the house and looked out over the dark valley. The moon had risen to the center of the sky and was now much smaller than the magnificent orb that had greeted the travelers earlier that evening. May took out a pack of cigarettes and lit one.

"This is the only time I allow myself a cigarette, when my children are asleep and Eventide is dark. Then I come out here and watch the stars and think about the day. Chuck called me a secret smoker. I think he was right. Aren't the stars beautiful, Jason?"

Jay looked upward and noticed for the first time that here, in a darkness more complete than he'd ever seen in the city, the stars seemed much brighter. It was a clear summer night. The evening air was cool, and except for an occasional grumble from a sleeping boy in the dormitory and a dog barking in the distance, Eventide was still.

"Now I understand why Chuck was away for so long. He had many other grandchildren to take care of. He didn't want to waste his time with a spoiled, rich one."

126

"You mustn't be bitter, Jason. I often thought there were demons chasing Chuck. He never seemed to slow down, and when he did he would get irritable and frustrated. He didn't forget you, and he spoke of you often. Why do you think he wanted to go back to Observatory after he'd had his stroke? It was the hardest moment in my life. I wanted him to stay here. I pleaded with him not to go back. I promised to take care of him. I said that he didn't have a life back there anymore, that his life was here among us and the home we'd created. He was almost paralyzed, but he was adamant and insisted I take him back to Cape Town. I'm sure you know how fierce he could be, even after his stroke."

"He would chase me out of the room when he couldn't speak any longer," Jason said, remembering the shell of a man, red with frustration, spittle running down his chin, turning his head angrily from side to side.

"Chuck wanted to get to know you. Before he left he told me that he knew it was too late, but that he had to try to reach you. It was the saddest I'd ever seen him. It was as if suddenly death had caught up with him and wasn't allowing him the time to finish what he needed to do. I couldn't insist that he stay, and I let him go knowing I'd never see him again."

May fell silent, drew on her cigarette, and exhaled slowly, the smoke just visible in the still night air.

Jay rested his head against the wall and tried to imagine what that farewell must have been like for the woman by his side. He glanced at her profile as she inhaled again, and the ember of the cigarette briefly lit up her face. She was staring into the distance, lost in her thoughts. The tang of tobacco suddenly reminded Jay of his father.

"Did I tell you my father bought a motorbike and has disappeared with a student from the University of Cape Town? My mother is terrified that this Watson habit of running off is in my genes and that I'll do the same one day."

"I wouldn't worry about it, Jason. There's nothing forcing you to do what they did. It's a choice your grandfather and your father made for themselves. Chuck was very angry with his sons. They had disappointed him in some way. I knew it had to do with the business he left them to run, but there was also something else much darker, which he never spoke about. He hardly ever mentioned his elder son."

" 'Peter, Peter, Pumpkin Eater, had a wife and couldn't keep her,' " Jay murmured, remembering the afternoon in Camps Bay and the moon card he had selected.

I was waiting for something back then, but now I'm searching, on the move. What did he say: The card is full of confusion, anxiety, and bewilderment?

" 'He put her in a pumpkin shell and there he kept her very well,' " May said, finishing the rhyme.

"I always think of my half uncle when I hear that rhyme. It's as if my family is living trapped in his great big pumpkin shell. I'm sorry, I'm not making any sense. May, you've probably guessed why I've come here, and I already know what you're going to say. You don't have Chuck's box, do you?"

"Jason, I'm sorry, but when the box was brought to Eventide I knew it wasn't for me to keep. Chuck had said if it should ever come to me, I should take it to Klasie right away. Klasie would know what to do with it. I must say I was tempted to break into it and see what Chuck had kept hidden from me all that time, but in the end I didn't. If Chuck had wanted to share it with me, he would have done so when he was alive. So last week I drove up to Knysna and dropped it off with Klasie."

"Who's Klasie?"

"He was the one who helped your grandfather catch one of the Knysna elephants and sell it to the circus. I think he's Chuck's oldest friend, and he lives in the Knysna forest. Your journey isn't quite over yet, I'm afraid."

"I didn't think it would be, somehow. Chuck left his mark on everyone he knew. Since I've been looking for the box, I've found out something about my family each step of the way, and I'm also finding out something about myself. Do you know, May, I was terrified about leaving school and facing the world this year? Everything was so safe at home in Observatory. I could have carried on like that for some time. Confronting my uncle, going into Khayelitsha, meeting you have done something for me."

"Good. I'm glad. That's the way it should be."

The two sat in companionable silence while May finished her cigarette.

When Jay stifled a yawn, May stood up.

"Well, it's time for bed. Wait here while I lock up."

May went into the house to fetch a flashlight, and Jay stood up and walked over to the center of the clearing. He gazed at the stars and the moon. The evening was at that special moment when everything was perfectly still.

I feel like I'm floating above the earth. Rising high above Eventide, becoming somebody else. This is a moment I won't ever forget. Gramps, I feel you around me. This is your place, you built it, lived here, you were loved here, and it's probably the closest I'm ever going to get to you.

Looking up at the sky, his head thrown back, Jay slowly turned around and around. He spun until the stars became a flickering kaleidoscope of swirling light. Still spinning, he opened his arms, their weight pulling him around and around. Finally, when he could spin no longer, he collapsed in a heap on the ground, panting and dizzy. He tried to get up but fell back to the ground.

And then, uncontrollably, tears came: Somewhere inside of him he was able to laugh at himself crying, lying in the dust, so dizzy he couldn't stand up. He lay flat and gazed skyward. The tears rolled down his cheeks and into his ears; slowly the sky stopped moving, and the stars steadied in their places.

Why so afraid, Jay-o? Yes, you're leaving home soon, but that's not going to kill you. You'll find something to do. There's so much I want, but I don't know what. And it has to be here, in this stupid, beautiful country. It has to be here! You're raving now, Jay-o, you're raving, and you look bloody stupid lying in the dust . . .

Jay hauled himself up from the ground, suddenly conscious of how absurd he must look, but there was no one around to see him. The buildings were dark. Behind the dormitory he saw the flicker of May's flashlight as she made her final rounds of the property. He sat down on the bench again and waited for her.

"Goodnight, Jason," May said as she came around the corner. "I hope you'll be comfortable in the dormitory."

"I'm sure I will. May, I want to thank you for everything this evening. For telling me so much about . . ."

"Hush." She smiled at him. "It's not necessary. Let's be friends, Jason. I'd like you to come visit me again. By yourself. Come and spend some time at Eventide, get to know the children, and we'll talk, some more."

Jay reached out and clumsily embraced May Eventide. For the brief moment he held her in his arms he felt how frail she was.

I will get to know you, May Eventide, before you go too. That's a promise I make to myself.

With no further words the two parted, and Jay went into the dark dormitory, crawled under the blankets on the bed his grandfather had made, and fell into a deep, sound sleep.

Dreams: a naked woman in a floppy hat sitting on a chair; unable to move, I drown in a tropical fish tank, but Chuck's gnarled hand grips mine, pulls me out, and he whispers, "Find the golden fleece, Jason."

"Hey, Jay, why so quiet?"

The Ark sped along the empty highway on its journey yet farther away from Cape Town. Andy was driving, while Mr. Lottee sat in the passenger seat enjoying the sweep of air through the open window and the warmth of the sun on his arm. Levi, in his usual place between driver and passenger, was looking ahead deep in thought. Lungile, Jay, and Carol sat in the back, talking.

"I'm just thinking, Carol. I had strange dreams last night."

"Me too, but then I always have funny dreams after a couple of tots of the Ole Brown."

"Carol, what do you want to do with your life?"

"Don't ask me that. I hate that question."

"You, Lungile?"

"My father wants me to study medicine, but I don't know if my marks are good enough for that."

"But what do *you* want to do," Jay insisted.

"I don't know. I don't like being asked that question either."

"Yeah, I know what you mean, but I can't help thinking about it all the time. I've finished school, I've got my examination results, and now I don't know what I want to do. Everything's so easy when you're at school. You don't have to think about anything but going to class, doing your homework, and writing exams. When you leave you suddenly find you have to live by different rules."

"Why do you think I travel around so much? I don't want to buy into all of that rubbish. I want to be as young as I am for a couple of years still."

"It's easy for you, Carol, because you're a woman."

"Rubbish! Why should I wait around for a man to take care of me? Isn't that copping out too? It's as hard for me as it is for you. It's very tempting just to sit around waiting for a rich husband—not that I'm going to find one in the circles I hang around in—and not do anything with your life. Okay, maybe it would be great to live the easy life as a rich wife to someone, but it also could be such a waste. That's something I think about all the time."

"There are so many different careers to choose from. How do you know which one is going to be right for you?" Jay pondered.

"You don't, and that's the problem. I'd rather not think about it. Sometimes I want to go and learn how to make jewelry properly, but then it seems such a big deal, and anyway I get by with what I sell. So I end up doing nothing, and just go up and down the coast."

"Look at May," Lungile said. "She didn't know she was going to run an orphanage until she was about fifty. It took her all those years to discover what she really wanted to do with her life."

They had left Eventide after an exuberant breakfast out in the sunshine with the children. Folding tables had been put up in a courtyard behind the buildings, and when the Ark's passengers awoke, they found a breakfast of porridge, thick slices of bread, and fresh milk waiting for them.

The children's familiar morning routine had been turned into an occasion by the presence of the visitors. Jay was guest of honor and was placed at the head of the table, where his grandfather used to sit. The food was served up, but before any of the children began eating all faces turned to Jay. May told him that Chuck had always said grace, and so Jay offered a prayer of thanks for the food before them. When he finished the children sang a hymn and then without further ceremony tucked into their porridge. Some of the older children asked Jay questions about his grandfather, many of which he couldn't answer. Many of the children had stories to tell about Chuck: how he had set someone's arm, built a go-cart, thrashed someone for breaking all the windows in the dormitory. They brought out an empty tropical fish tank: That was where Chuck had kept his goldfish. They showed Jay the book of Greek myths for children from which Chuck had read to them. Some clamored for Jay to read to them then and there, but May intervened, distracting the children by putting a bowl of sugar on the table as a special treat.

After breakfast the friends were shown around Eventide, which by day was considerably smaller than it had seemed the night before. May gave Jay directions on how to get to Klasie, and after everyone promised to return to Eventide someday, he and his friends rather reluctantly set off on the road again.

The problem was Levi's mother. She had to be told they were staying another day. In Mossel Bay Levi and Jay tried to phone her, but still there was no reply from her house. Instead, Jay phoned Margaret and explained their new plans to her.

Once out of the town, everyone bubbled over into discussing Eventide.

"But May is special, Lungile," Andy called out from the driver's seat. "She's an extraordinary woman: There can't be many people like her."

"She's only extraordinary because everyone else is so self-centered. She's looking after children that nobody wants. That's not such a unique thing in itself. In fact, it's quite a simple idea, but because so many other people are only concerned about careers and making money and getting somewhere in life, we think it is extraordinary," Carol said.

"But everyone can't adopt an unwanted child," Andy responded.

"Why not? It wouldn't be such a bad idea."

"I think it's a great idea," Levi said.

"You're an idealist, Carol. People are just not like that," Lungile insisted.

"When I was young I always knew what I was going to do with my life," said Mr. Lottee, joining the conversation. "My father was a bookbinder, and I never questioned that I would be one, too, someday. It was as simple as that. But nowadays that isn't how things work, and young people are running around all over the place not knowing what to do. It seems the jobs your parents do are no longer good enough for you."

"Well, who wants to be an insurance salesman?" Andy asked.

"Exactly, or run a pet shop—badly," Jay added.

"Or be a nurse. Yuggh!"

"I don't ever want to be anything!" Levi said, topping Carol's exclamation of disgust with a double *yuggh*.

"But it's not what you do, it's how you do it," Mr. Lottee said. "Look at your grandfather, Jay. He built his pet empire, and it was the most important thing in his life. He put everything into it."

"But then he walked out on it all, as if everything he had achieved had become meaningless."

"And my grandfather committed suicide," Andy said bitterly.

While its occupants were busy discussing their futures, the Ark sped along the highway and through the small sea-side town of Wilderness. On both sides of the road the vegetation was dense with climbing vines, birch trees, and shrubby bushes. It was just after noon and halfway between Wilderness and Rondevlei that the Ark decided to stir up some trouble. The old van was pounding up a steep hill. Andy, anxious to get to Knysna, was pushing her a little over the speed limit. The engine jerked, spluttered, recovered, spluttered again, and died. Andy swore and pulled her off the road. As soon as the van came to a stop he jumped out to look under the hood. Using their few tools, he could not find out what was wrong, so, after turning the van around, they freewheeled back down the hill trying to start the engine. It didn't catch. The Ark floundered to a stop at the bottom of the hill, thirty kilometers away from the nearest town.

"So what do we do now?" Jay asked as they all stood around on the side of the road looking miserable while Andy took one last look at the engine. His hands were covered with grease and his face was smudged. He shook his head in despair and slammed down the hood.

"I just don't know what it is! It must be something that will have to be fixed at a garage."

"Why don't Andy and I go into Wilderness and get a pickup truck to tow us in?" Jay suggested wearily.

"If I just had the right tools!"

"Hey, take it easy, Andy, you've done everything you could. It's nobody's fault."

"Carol, you're not going to leave now?" Levi said, staring hard at the young woman. "You can't go. It won't take long to get the Ark fixed, and there's Jay's box. You want to see what's inside it, too, don't you?" Levi was desperate. "Please stay."

"You think I'd leave because the old jalopy dies on us? Relax, Levi. These guys are going to need someone who knows how to hitchhike. Besides, I don't think they know this area as well as I do. Isn't that right?"

"What do you mean?" Jay asked, exasperated by Carol.

"Let's face it. We're not going to get to Klasie today."

Everyone groaned at Carol's words.

"By the time we get the Ark back to Wilderness it will be three in the afternoon. It will take at least two to three hours to fix it, and then we've still got another hour and a half driving to Knysna—"

"And remember May said the walk in the forest to Klasie takes about forty minutes," Mr. Lottee interjected. "And then we would have to drive back to Cape Town in the dark."

"I'd forgotten that, but Mr. Lottee's right. So that means we'll be wandering around the Knysna forest after dark. No thanks! Look, I know a place outside Wilderness where we can spend the night, and I suggest we leave early tomorrow morning for Knysna," Carol said.

"Carol's right. I agree," said Levi.

"Don't look so upset, Jay. Let's go and sort it out. She's right. We're not going to make Knysna today," Andy added, impatient to get on to the next town and find an emergency pickup truck.

"How much money have we got among us? This could cost a lot."

"I've got my cash card," Lungile said.

"I've brought mine too. I'll pay everyone back when we get home," Jay promised, and collected what he needed to hitchhike to the next town.

"All right, let's hit the road," Carol said. "Come on, Levi. You're going to be our ticket into Wilderness. Nobody can resist a little angel like you!"

An hour later a tow truck appeared down the road, and by a quarter to three that afternoon the Ark had been towed into a garage in Wilderness. The van was put up on a jack, and Andy and the mechanic immediately started working. The others strolled around Wilderness, looked into shop windows, and walked up and down the main street a couple of times.

"I'm worried about Levi's mother. This will be the second night we haven't come home," Mr. Lottee said.

"I left a message with my mother, and anyway Jenny knows where to find out about us, doesn't she, Levi?"

The boy shrugged and grinned maliciously.

"What're you grinning at, you Cheshire cat?"

"I don't want to phone her. I want her to worry."

"Levi!" Jay groaned. "Carol, please won't you make sure Levi phones his mother and tells her what has happened?"

"Come on, Terror, you and I are going shopping. Can I have some contributions for supper tonight, please?" Carol said. "We'll see you back at the garage in an hour. Lungile, won't you buy some charcoal?" Taking Levi's hand, she strolled off in search of a public telephone.

"That little fellow is stuck on Carol," Mr. Lottee commented as they watched the two walk away.　　•

"I've never seen him like this. When he's with his mother, he's quite different," Jay replied. "Okay, who's for a game of cards. Lungile? Mr. Lottee?"

"I think I'll just buy a newspaper and have a cup of tea. You and Lungile carry on," Mr. Lottee said and wandered off to buy a newspaper. For the rest of the afternoon he sat and read his paper at the garage while the boys played cards.

At six o'clock—and four hundred rands poorer—they were on the road again. The Ark purred beneath them as if nothing had ever been wrong. Twenty minutes outside of the town of Wilderness they pulled off the highway. Following Carol's directions, they headed into the forest.

"It's just a little farther," Carol said as the Ark bumped along the dirt track. In the distance they could hear the sound of water. Then the Ark rounded a corner, and Mr. Lottee pulled up alongside the tallest, thickest tree they had ever seen.

"The Great Tree!" Carol announced as everyone got out of the van and walked around its huge girth.

"And a waterfall," Lungile shouted, pointing to a sheet of water falling into a deep pool some distance from the clearing.

"Well, what do you think of my secret campsite?" Carol asked proudly.

"It's perfect," Jay shouted, and he began stripping off his clothes, to the bewilderment of the others.

Head for the water, Jay-o. Time to feel the water all around again. Splash! Mountain ice. Sparkling clean, smelling of pines, moss, and wood smoke.

Before nightfall, a campfire was roaring in the clearing, and Carol and Levi were organizing supper. While they opened tinned fruit, salted the meat, and wrapped potatoes in tinfoil they seemed to be in deep conversation, and whenever anyone approached to help out they declined the offer.

Mr. Lottee and Lungile had taken boxes out from the back of the van and placed them around the fire to sit on. Andy and Jay had put up the small two-man tent they had brought along and laid out the blankets and sleeping bags. Everyone was hungry, and Levi proudly announced, as he served the first meal he had ever prepared, that he wanted to be a chef when he grew up. After they had eaten and the fire had died down, Mr. Lottee told them stories about Turkey, but soon the conversation returned to Jay's grandfather and what they might find at Klasie's.

Once again Levi was the first to fall asleep. Carol carried him to the van and put him to bed. When she returned, Mr. Lottee had retired to the tent with Lungile, and Andy was preparing his sleeping bag beside the van.

Carol sat down next to Jay, who had thrown the remainder of the charcoal on the fire. There was a comfortable, fire-watching silence between them until Carol spoke.

"I nearly had a child once. I'm sure he would have been just like Levi," she said, staring into the glowing embers.

"You did?" Jay said, surprised.

"An unwanted present from a drummer in a rock band. I was too young. Or at least I thought I was, last year. But now I don't know. I look at Levi and I sometimes think what a terrible mistake I made." She stopped suddenly, gathered some sand in her hands, and threw it onto the fire. "He's a strange boy."

"There never was a stranger fish," Jay said, as the darkness of the forest fell upon the Ark and its passengers.

THE SUN HAD BARELY RISEN as the Ark approached the outskirts of Knysna. Before they came to the town, they took a road that led them away from the sea and up into Phantom Pass. Stinkwood and yellowwood trees towered over the Ark as the travelers entered the deepest part of the Knysna forest.

As they drove farther into the back country, they saw fewer and fewer houses. The tarred road became a dusty track and then hardly more than an overgrown path.

"Who on earth lives out here?" Carol wondered.

The air was heavy with the scent of the forest: sticky pines, burning wood, and decaying leaves.

"I can see how easily your grandfather could have disappeared in this forest," said Andy.

He slowed the van down while Lungile and Jay got out to move a branch that was blocking the way.

What were you doing so deep in the forest, Gramps? May said you spent a lot of time up here. Why?

The travelers' ears rang with the high-pitched trill of millions of cicadas. Once the way was cleared, they drove on until the path finally ended in a grassy dead end.

Andy switched off the engine, and everyone, eager to stretch after the two-hour drive, climbed out of the van.

"May said this is what we'd find. Now we have to look for a footpath," said Jay. They all spread out around the small clearing and hunted for a path leading deeper into the forest.

"Here it is!" Levi called triumphantly.

Mr. Lottee looked doubtfully down the path.

"I think somebody should stay with the van," he said, "and I'm volunteering. I didn't bring my hiking shoes. Levi, you should stay here too."

"No! I want to go," said Levi, clutching Carol's hand.

"I'll look after him," Carol said, as each looked at the others, waiting for someone to offer to stay with Mr. Lottee.

Finally Andy said, "I'll wait with you."

"Let's go," Jay urged, eager to set off into the forest. "Lungile, put some oranges in the rucksack. I'll carry the water bottle."

"Jay, we must get back to Cape Town today," said Mr. Lottee. "It's eight o'clock now. If we leave at ten we should make it by late afternoon."

"I'll try and be as quick as I can," Jay responded.

And if Klasie doesn't have the box? No, don't think like that. He'll have it.

The group followed the path into the forest, which seemed to close in behind them as they walked along. Shafts of sunlight fell at different angles through the trees, but there were places where the leaves overhead blocked out the sun entirely and the forest was dark.

The path crossed other small tracks and wound back on itself several times. Sometimes it was hard to distinguish one path from another: They all looked equally well trodden. The number of paths suggested this part of the forest was not so uninhabited as it had appeared at first.

"And now?" Jay said, as the path petered out.

"Perhaps it goes on over here," Lungile said, walking a little way into the forest. The others spread out to look for the path.

"Don't go too far away," Jay shouted. "I don't want anyone to get lost."

"Let's ask that old man," Levi said. The others turned

141

around to where he was pointing. The forest had grown still.

"Who?" Carol said, peering into the green thickness of the surrounding undergrowth.

"He was standing under that tree, watching us," Levi said, and moved quickly to where he had pointed. The others followed him.

"It's only a bush, Levi," Lungile said. "You must have imagined it."

Levi walked around the tree. "Here's the path," he said, pointing to a clear track moving deeper into the forest.

"Way to go!" Jay said, slapping Levi on the back. The boy smiled and led the others on the new track he had found.

They had been walking for about half an hour when, through a gap in the trees, they saw a thin wisp of gray smoke rising above the forest.

"It looks like someone's at home," Jay said.

"I'm hungry," complained Levi.

"Me, too," said Carol.

"Have an orange." Lungile swung the pack around and handed out the fruit. They continued walking while they peeled their oranges.

After a short while they came to a wooden hut standing in a large clearing. Beside the hut ran a stream bridged by two planks. There were raw tree stumps scattered around the clearing, and next to the hut was an open shed whose floor was covered with wood chips. Some distance away stood a third dilapidated building, its door hanging open and its windowpanes cracked.

As they were looking around them an old colored man came across the makeshift bridge. He stopped when he saw the strangers. He was carrying a newly slaughtered chicken, which was still jerking sporadically.

"What are you people doing here?" he barked.

He was wearing a rough shirt and a pair of scruffy

brown trousers too big for his skeletal frame. White stubble stuck out from his pointed chin, but except for a few white tufts on the side of his head he was bald. He wore no shoes, and his feet were large and calloused.

Jay stepped forward. "We're looking for Klasie."

"This is private property. You're trespassing." The old man repeated his question. "What are you doing here?" Forgetting the headless bird in his hand, he shook it at the company. "This is private property."

"It's got no head," Levi whispered to Carol. "But it's still wriggling."

"My name is Jay Watson. May Eventide sent me and—"

"What?" the old man shouted, moving toward Jay. "What did you say?"

"We're looking for Klasie," Carol shouted.

At last the old man seemed to understand something. "Klasie! Who wants Klasie?"

"I think he's a bit deaf, Jay," Carol said under her breath.

"Huh, what did she say? Deaf! No way! I can still hear as good as anyone. Who wants Klasie?"

"My name is Jay Watson. I'm the grandson of Chuck. Chuck Watson!" Jay shouted.

"No bloody way! You've got to be kidding! You the kid? You can't be! You're almost a man. How old are you?"

"Seventeen."

"Let me see," the old man muttered to himself, closing his eyes as he mentally totted up the years. After a moment he opened his eyes and grinned at Jay. "That's about right. Man, how time flies! I remember when you were a snot-nosed kid, this high." The man indicated a height below his knees and chuckled. "Same hair. I'm Klasie! Don't you remember me?"

Jay shook his head and introduced his companions to his grandfather's old friend.

"If I knew you were all coming I would have cooked some chicken liver and onions—"

143

Jay could no longer contain himself. He had only one question to ask, and he had to know the answer to it immediately.

"Klasie, do you have Chuck's yellowwood box?"

"Ahh, ja, man, so that's the reason you came?"

"Yes. Do you have it?"

"May brought it to me a couple of weeks ago."

"Do you have it here, in that hut?"

"Yes, of course I do. Where else am I going to keep it?"

Jay wanted to shout wildly, he wanted to lift the old man and swing him around, he wanted to dance across the grass, do a handspring. Instead he smiled and turned to the others. "At last!"

"Why do you want it?" Klasie asked suspiciously.

"Chuck left it to me. He wanted me to have it." Jay explained the saga of the search for the box once again. When he got to the part about Khayelitsha, Klasie interrupted him.

"So Arthur is dead, hey? I told him I'd outlive him! Ja, Arthur, you thought you would live longer than me. That'll be the bloody day!" he shouted jubilantly and then let Jay continue telling his story.

"So you've gone on a real goosie chase to find old Klasie? Chuck was a clever chap. I'm damn sure he wanted you to do just that," Klasie said with a chuckle. "Well, come inside. No, hang on," he said as they moved forward. "I don't think I can fit all of you inside. I'm just a bachelor and there's only room for one."

Lungile, Levi, and Carol waited outside while Klasie took Jay into his hut. Inside it was cool and dark. Shafts of sunlight arrowed through the holes in the wooden slat walls. The hut smelled of smoke, burned meat, and stale wine. Klasie kicked a few empty wine bottles into a corner and cleared the table.

"May said Chuck spent a lot of time here, Klasie. What was he doing?"

"Working."

"Working at what?"

"Remembering his life. Ja, those were his words: 'Klasie, I'm going to remember my life and I'm going to do it here.' "

From under his bed Klasie pulled out a suitcase and then got down on his knees to reach for something farther back near the wall.

"He lived in that other shed, and some days he would never come out of it. Sometimes he would go for long walks in the forest, but most times he would spend the day in the shed working. Ahh, here it is!"

Jay got down on his knees beside Klasie to help him pull out Chuck Watson's last gift to his grandson.

The box was a little bigger than a shoe box but smaller than a trunk. The wood was smooth, with a golden-brown sheen. Klasie pulled out his handkerchief and gave the top a quick rub. The box had no handles; it had brass hinges and a lock.

Jay found he could not touch it at first. For a few minutes he looked down at the box before them on the ground; then he laid his hand gently on the lock.

It's a very ordinary box. What were you expecting, Jay-o? Did you want lights to flash? This wooden box was important to Chuck—so important that his closest friends kept it safe for him after his death. That should be enough.

Jay could not help feeling disappointed. The taxing journey they had made deserved a better reward than this old wooden box. He was ashamed to go outside and show the others this very ordinary object.

"Can I open it?" he asked, finally lifting the box and placing it upon the table.

"Yes, yes, of course. The key's around here somewhere."

Klasie threw some clothes about as he scrabbled for the key. "Ag no, man! Where's that damn key now?" He rifled

145

through the jars, cups, and bottles on the window ledge. He opened a wooden chest and threw out a rubber boot, tattered *Scope* magazines, an old musket, a brass kettle, animal traps, and a ruined hot-water bottle.

Carol and Levi stood in the doorway and peered into the gloom of the hut. "Did we find it?" Levi asked.

"Here it is," said Jay, resting his hand on the box.

"What's inside?" Carol asked as she stepped into the hut. Lungile moved forward so that he, too, could see into the room.

"I don't know. He can't find the key!"

Everybody piled into the hut to look for the missing key. Klasie had begun pulling up loose floorboards, while Lungile and Carol sorted through the clothes, papers, bottles, pots, and pans that had been flung haphazardly around the room.

"I put it in a safe place! That's how it always is. Safe places are lost places!" Klasie said, swearing under his breath.

"Here it is!" Levi called out triumphantly as he took a key off a nail behind the door.

"Ahh, there's the little beggar!" Klasie snatched the key from Levi and came over to the table, solemnly handing the key to Jay.

"You open it, Jason. It hasn't been open since Chuck died."

Feeling a little foolish, Jay slipped the key into the rusty lock and with a little difficulty unlocked the box. He lifted the lid and looked inside. A faint moldy smell came from within.

"Papers. It's full of papers."

Jay pulled out thick sheaves of paper covered with writing and placed them on the table. Some of the pages had been neatly copied out, the writing on others was an illegible scribble, while some were heavily scrawled over with red ink.

"They're not just papers, they're Chuck's stories," Klasie said indignantly.

"Is that all?" Carol said, disappointed, and articulating what the others were all wondering.

"I don't know. I'll have to go through it carefully. What was my grandfather doing with all this, Klasie?"

"Years ago Arthur Jacobs put some stupid idea into his head, which really spooked him badly. I'd known Chuck for a long time. I helped him catch a forest elephant and other big game when he was running his animal business. He was the most level-headed and straightforward guy you could ask for. Then one day he suddenly got this crazy idea into his head. Arthur Jacobs was to blame, but Chuck said he'd thought about it long before Arthur had spoken to him."

Klasie spoke slowly, impressively, emphasizing each word, looking from one to the other as he recalled the crucial change in Chuck Watson's life.

"Man, him and Arthur started talking about life and death. I called it drunk men's conversations. Anyway, Chuck asked Arthur what he believed in. Arthur tells him there's nothing after you die but the story of your life, and what good is a story if it's not worth telling. After he had been speaking to Arthur, Chuck would say to me that he hadn't any story to leave behind, that when he died nobody would remember him. Chuck said that he'd been wasting time, and nothing he had done in his life seemed worthwhile. I said to him that it was just one of those damn-fool ideas white people have and he should forget all about it and have a drink, but he didn't find that funny."

"And so he disappeared for ten years to live his life over again?"

"Why do you sound so angry? That's not a bad idea. Who wouldn't want to do that? He wasn't going to live his life over, but just live what was left better. He met May Eventide and bought some land to build a home for poor

147

kids. He wanted to do something special he could write about. How can I write if I don't live, he would ask. His big dream was to be published in hardback. Hardback, that was his dream: Chuck's stories in hardback. So when I retired he came here and wrote. He wrote every bloody day, sitting in that cabin and writing his heart out. Some of the stories he wrote were about his travels, some were about his life, but all of them were about South Africa. He read bits of them to me, but he could never finish any of them. Some would start out really fine, but when I asked him what had happened in the end he would already be on to the next story. And when he wasn't writing he would be at Eventide. I told him to marry May and make an honest woman of her, but he said he couldn't completely break his ties with his family in Cape Town. He said his wife was going senile and that he couldn't remarry until she died."

"But that didn't stop him from staying away. He only came back when he had to because of his stroke."

"You don't understand, boy. Chuck had found his life's work and he had a lot to do. 'Hardback, Klasie,' he would say. 'Hardback is what real writers publish.' Ja, I was sorry when he had that stroke. There were so many unfinished stories. But maybe that's why he wanted you to have them. That's it! He wanted you to get them published for him." Klasie picked up some of the papers and held them out to Jay. "Maybe you can take them to a publisher and see what he thinks. They're good, man."

Unfinished tatters of a useless life. Chuck-a-luck, Chuck-a-luck, what were you trying to do? How was an illegible scrawl across hundreds of white pages going to save you?

Waves of disappointment swept over Jay as he stared at the papers in his hands.

"Well, that's it, folks. We've traveled hundreds of miles for the unfinished, illegible stories of my grandfather. I'm sorry there isn't anything more exciting to show you," Jay said, throwing the papers back into the box and slamming the lid.

"What the hell do you know?" Klasie bellowed at Jay, startling him. "You didn't see him sitting there day in, day out, writing until he fell asleep at his table. I would come in to put out the lamp. This was the most precious thing in his life."

"I'm not denying it was important to him," said Jay hastily, "but he's dead now and it's all over. He just left a mass of unfinished work that got nowhere!"

"You haven't read any of it yet," Lungile reminded Jay from the doorway. "Maybe some of it's good."

"Get out! Get out!" The old man banged the table with his open hand. "You show no respect for your dead grandfather. Shame on you!"

Jay, who had picked up the box, dispiritedly walked out of the hut.

Shout all you like, old man. Nothing can touch me anymore. Goosie chase, you called it. You're damn right!

"Come on, let's go," he said, crossing the open space outside the hut.

"Jay! Wait!" Lungile said, running after him. "You can't just leave like that. Don't you want to see where your grandfather lived? That's the cabin Klasie was talking about." He pointed at the dilapidated hut a distance from the clearing.

'It's just an old, run-down shack. Come on, we're going back to Cape Town."

Carol tried to pacify the angry old man. He was standing in the doorway of the hut bellowing curses after Jay, who, followed by Lungile, was rapidly disappearing into the forest. Eventually, worn out, Klasie turned back into the hut and slammed the door on Carol and Levi. They had no choice but to follow Jay and Lungile back to the Ark.

Jay stormed out of the forest and threw the box into the

back of the van. Until the others arrived he fended off the eager questions of Mr. Lottee and Andy as best he could. Yes, he had found the box, no, there was nothing in it, only old papers. When Carol and Levi appeared Jay turned to Mr. Lottee. "You wanted to get back to Cape Town, so let's go. I've got what I came for," he said curtly, barely able to restrain the inexplicable fury he felt.

"You could at least have heard him out, Jay, instead of storming out of there like a spoiled child who hadn't been given his lollipop," said Carol, shutting the sliding door as Mr. Lottee pulled away.

"Carol, I don't want to talk about it!"

"I want to see what's in the box," said Levi.

"Leave it alone, Levi! Don't touch it!"

"Calm down, calm down. There's no need to shout," Mr. Lottee said, raising his own voice.

Jay took a deep breath and stared morosely out of the window at the passing forest. The group drove in silence until they had left the Knysna forest behind. The road back seemed shorter than it had on the outward journey, and soon they had reached the highway. Jay had calmed down slightly and managed somehow to join in the conversation, which limped along, touching on anything but the forest, Klasie, or the box.

Before they entered the on-ramp to Cape Town, Mr. Lottee stopped the van and looked over at Carol.

"I guess this is where I say good-bye," Carol said as she gave Levi a hug and leaned over for her rucksack.

"Carol, I'm sorry I was so rude back there."

"Hey, don't apologize to me, Jay. I don't care. You have to apologize to Klasie," she said, getting out of the van.

Levi got out with her and stood at the side of the road.

"And where do you think you're going?" Jay asked.

"I'm not going back to Cape Town. I'm going with Carol," Levi said stonily.

"Levi," Carol said softly, "I told you last night. You can't come with me."

"I have to. This is my only chance, Carol. I have to come with you! I can't go back. Don't make me go back." Jay climbed out of the van and went up to him. Levi backed away, his eyes wide with anger and fear.

"Old man, you can't just go. It doesn't work like—"

"Why not? I have to. Jay, I have to. Don't make me!" the boy shouted, clinging to Carol's hand. Tears ran down his cheeks. She tried to disengage herself, but he wouldn't let her go. Jay looked helplessly at the distraught boy.

Carol gestured to Jay to back off as she knelt beside Levi. Turning him gently toward her, she stroked the hair away from his eyes. She whispered to him as he looked at her, his hands resting on her shoulders. Levi sobbed in gulps, trying to check his tears. He shook his head vigorously, his eyes closed, as Carol continued whispering to him.

Mr. Lottee switched the motor off and climbed down onto the road.

"He can't go with her, Jay," he said softly.

"I know that, Mr. Lottee. Of course he can't. But the little guy doesn't understand that."

The friends waited patiently while Carol talked to Levi at the side of the highway. Finally, the boy turned abruptly away from her and walked determinedly back to the van. His face was pale and strained. Without looking at anyone, he climbed into the van and crawled into one of the larger cages.

"Go quickly, Jay, before he changes his mind," Carol whispered, close to tears herself. "Bye, everyone. Thanks for the ride."

She walked a little way up the road and turned to wave as Mr. Lottee swung out on the highway back to Cape Town.

They drove for the rest of the day, only stopping for petrol and a brief lunch. No one could cajole Levi to leave the cage he had crawled into. He lay curled up in the corner, not speaking to anyone, and occasionally they heard him muttering the name David Leviticus Howard to himself, over and over.

Jay stared dismally out at the countryside and contemplated taking to the road in the same way his father had done. His thoughts were jumbled, apart from the single dominant idea that somewhere along the way he must have taken a wrong turn.

The box lay neglected in the back of the Ark. Nobody mentioned it or its contents, and Jay ignored it. He still felt uncomfortable about having dragged so many people around the countryside in pursuit of something that had turned out to be only a lot of old papers.

In the distance the Hottentots Holland mountain range rose up as they neared their journey's end. They reached the top of Sir Lowry's Pass at four o'clock, and below them the spread of the vineyards, the village of Somerset West, False Bay, and the Cape Flats led their eyes to the distant bulk of Table Mountain. Lungile wanted to stop and look at the view, but everyone else was tired and wanted to get home, and so the Ark went sailing down the pass.

Once past Somerset West Mr. Lottee mentioned for the first time what had taken them away from Cape Town. "What are you going to do now, Jay? You've got what you were looking for."

"I don't know if I have, though."

Jay turned around to Lungile at the back. "Pass me that box, will you, Lungile?"

Lungile passed the box to the front. Jay put it on his lap. The wood was smooth to his touch, and although the box was roughly made, he had to admit it was rather beautiful. He ran his hand over the lid.

Disappointed, yes. But I've done the right thing, Chuck. You wanted me to have it, and now I've got your precious treasure.

As Table Mountain came into view he felt unexpectedly at peace with the outcome of his travels.

The Ark pulled into Observatory at five-thirty, and its passengers, grateful to be home at last, piled out of the van. Although travel weary, they were reluctant to break up and were slow about unpacking their gear from the back of the van.

"Levi, you'd better go home," Jay said, when the van was finally empty and the others had gone.

The boy had not left the cage and was still sitting as he had done for most of the journey, staring in front of him with his arms folded.

"I don't want to go home. I want to stay in the Ark forever," he announced defiantly.

Jay went around to the back of the van and looked at the boy in the cage.

"Lee, old man, the journey's over," he said gently. "It's been a great adventure, but it's over now and we all have to go home."

"Jay . . ." Levi hesitated. "Will you come with me, please?"

It was the first time Jay had heard Levi use the word *please,* and he detected in the boy's words an urgency he could not ignore.

"Of course I'll come with you. What's wrong?"

There's something you're not telling me, old man. Why do you look frightened and pale?

"I just want you to come home with me."

Levi climbed out of the van and waited for Jay to lock it. They walked down Station Road. As they turned into Darien Square, Levi stopped dead.

The black truck was parked outside Jenny Bam's cottage.

"I'm not going in!"

Levi turned around and started walking quickly away. Jay lunged after him and grabbed his arm. When he turned Levi around he saw blind panic in his eyes.

"Levi?"

"I don't want to go in there! Can't you see he's there? He's there—waiting for me. I don't want to go. Not now!"

The boy was almost screaming as he struggled fiercely in Jay's grip.

"Levi, what's the matter with you? Tell me!"

The boy was trembling, his face ashen, and he seemed to look right through Jay.

"I don't want to go home. It's not right for me yet. I want to stay away longer. Don't make me!"

Jay crouched down in front of Levi, held him firmly by the shoulders, and looked sternly at him.

"Levi, did you speak to your mother when you phoned from Wilderness?"

The boy stared at Jay. His eyes had narrowed and there was no expression on his face.

"Did you?"

"No."

"Levi!"

"We had a fight on Sunday. She locked me in my room and said I couldn't go with you to Mossel Bay. I had to go. After they'd gone on Monday morning, I broke my window and climbed out."

"What! After she'd said you couldn't come with us?" Jay shook his head and knelt beside the boy.

"Levi, you've got to go home sooner or later, and we might as well get it over with now. Listen to me. We'll go in together, we'll explain everything, and it will be all right. Okay? Levi, look at me. Okay? You've got no choice, old man. Let's just get it over with."

"Get it over with," the boy repeated in a monotone.

Then, seemingly having resolved something within himself, he looked at Jay for a long moment.

What are you trying to tell me that doesn't come in words, Levi?

"Let's get it over with," the boy said again. He took Jay's hand and began walking with him toward his mother's cottage.

Levi held tightly onto Jay's hand as they opened the gate to the Bam cottage. His hand felt clammy and small, but he walked without hesitation up to the front door, opened it, and stepped inside. The house was quiet, and Jay felt the boy's grip relax slightly.

Levi went down the passage toward the kitchen, and Jay followed, closing the front door behind them.

Jenny Bam and Gary Martin were in the kitchen. On a plate in the center of the table were two large jam doughnuts. Gary was drinking coffee and reading a newspaper. Jenny was cutting out a pattern at the other end of the table. She paused, shears in one hand, doughnut in the other, when she caught sight of her son standing in the doorway.

"Levi! Where the hell have you been?"

Jay appeared in the doorway behind the boy and lamely greeted the two adults.

"Jay, what are you doing here?"

"I've come to explain what happened."

"So you've finally decided to come home," said Gary, putting his newspaper down and eyeing the boy balefully.

Levi's eyes flicked from his mother to her boyfriend, but he said nothing and stood motionless.

Jay edged past him into the room.

"We've been worried sick about you, Levi," Jenny said, putting down her shears and going to kneel in front of the boy.

It looks like it: coffee, jam doughnuts, and the afternoon papers.

Feeling he had to speak up on behalf of the silent boy, Jay opened his mouth . . .

I don't want to get involved. Why did I ever think to take the old man with us?

. . . and then shut it again.

"Levi?" Jenny said, waiting for her son to answer.

Everyone was looking at the boy. He would have seemed distracted or indifferent were it not for his eyes, which continually flicked back and forth between Jenny and Gary. He seemed to be assessing the gravity of the situation and weighing up his chances. His silence was cleverly calculated, frustrating the two adults, who were forced to wait, defeated by his refusal to engage in battle.

"Jenny, it's all my fault. The van broke down in Wilderness, and I had to go to Knysna . . ."

His voice trailed off as Gary Martin's gaze shifted momentarily in his direction.

"It's got nothing to do with you, kid," he said curtly and dismissively.

He turned back to Levi. "It's Denim over here who is a perverse little sod. You're going to have to pay for the tapes you trashed and the window you smashed, you know. Or is it just one more thing he's going to get away with?" This last was directed at Jenny, who ignored him.

Levi's eyes glazed over and narrowed. With no expression on his face he looked at his mother's boyfriend.

Leave. Don't get involved. You've said what you wanted to say. Now go.

"Jenny, I'm sorry." Jay spoke again, in an effort to deflect the pair's attention from Levi. He edged closer to the boy and nudged him, trying to make him react somehow.

Will you do something to save yourself, old man? Speak, anything. You're not helping by acting the catatonic!

"Didn't you know I'd forbidden Levi to go with you? He

157

was in one of his moods on Sunday morning and destroyed Gary's tape collection. Didn't he tell you?"

"No, he didn't, Jenny." Jay was shocked. "I wouldn't have let him come with us if I'd known that."

Levi flashed a withering glance at Jay.

You traitor, Jay-o. You bloody traitor! Sorry, old man.

"We tried to phone you on Tuesday morning, but there was no reply, and then I made him phone you from Wilderness. I thought he spoke to you then, but—"

"He didn't speak to me. You don't know him, Jay. He lies all the time."

Gary stood up and walked over to the boy.

"God knows why, but your mother's been worried sick about you. What have you got to say to her?" He grabbed Levi's arm and shook him.

The boy grunted. It was the sound of a small, cornered animal. He hung awkwardly twisted by Gary's grip on his arm and stared at his mother.

"Gary, let him go," she ordered. As the man obeyed her, she changed her tone and tried to reason with her son. "Levi, you know I said you couldn't go. Not after how you'd behaved on Sunday, and then you broke a window and went anyway. What did you expect me to do?"

"Your mother was about to contact the police."

"Didn't Margaret call you?" Jay asked, increasingly bewildered by the force of the anger directed at Levi.

"Margaret?"

"My mother."

Jenny shook her head.

"I spoke to her on Monday evening and told her to phone you about Levi. I thought that if you knew where he would be . . ."

"We didn't know he was gone until late Monday night," Gary said.

Jenny flushed at his admission and shot him an angry glance.

So you went to the beach on Monday anyway and left him locked in his room all day as punishment, and only came back late that night. No wonder he broke the window.

"Why didn't you at least leave a note or something?" she asked, directing her attention back to Levi.

Still Levi said nothing. Ignoring his mother, he turned to leave the kitchen.

"Oh no you don't." Gary put out his hand to stop him. "You're not going to get out of it so easily this time. What have you got to say for yourself, Levi? And don't try the silent treatment on us. It doesn't work."

"I don't need to talk to you, arsehole!" Levi suddenly shrilled straight into Gary's face.

The man's hand lashed out and struck the boy across the face.

"Gary!" Jenny screamed.

She moved quickly to pull her boyfriend away from Levi, who had been knocked back against the table. His eyes blazed, and a crimson mark on his cheek stood out against his pallor. He saw the shock on Jay's face.

So the corners in this house are belts and fists. Don't look at me like that, old man. I didn't see anything.

Levi's face registered excruciating shame at Jay's growing comprehension. He lowered his head to hide his frown from Jay. Then he raised it again to glare at Gary, who was trying to shake off Jenny's grasp.

"Don't hit him again, Gary. I've told you not to hit him!"

"He needs a good hiding! You're too soft on him, Jen."

"Don't you tell me what—"

Jay picked up only a blurred impression of Levi, shears in hand, launching himself at Gary Martin.

"Levi!" Jay yelled frantically, making a futile grab at the distraught boy. Gary turned in time to receive Levi's lunge, which drove the shears deep into his side.

For a moment Gary looked incredulous, and then with his full weight he struck out at Levi with his clenched fist. The blow caught the boy on the side of the chin, lifting him off his feet and across the room. His head caught the corner of the table, and he slid to the floor.

"Levi!" Jenny screamed and rushed over to him.

Desperately Gary jerked the shears out of his side and threw them across the room. Blood spattered around him as he ran for the bathroom.

"That crazy little shit stabbed me!" he yelled in disbelief as he rummaged through the linen cupboard for towels to stanch the bleeding.

Jay stood transfixed.

Jenny cradled Levi's head as she searched for a wound.

"Are you bleeding, baby? Does it hurt? Jay, phone for an ambulance. Gary!" she screamed. "Gary, where are the keys to the truck? We've got to get Levi to the hospital. He's out cold."

"What about me? I'm bleeding to death. How can I bloody well drive?" came the hysterical response from the bathroom.

Jay skidded down the passage to the phone and reported the accident. The ambulances were all out on calls; the operator said it would be quicker for them to bring the boy in themselves. When Jay came back Jenny had lifted Levi in her arms. She jerked her head at the keys, lying on the counter.

"Jay, the keys!"

Carrying Levi, she pushed past Jay down the passage.

How small you are, old man. How small.

"I'm coming with you," Gary called from behind them as

he came hobbling along the passage with a towel pressed to his bloodied side.

"You've killed him, Gary," Jenny sobbed as she carefully laid Levi down on the seat of the truck.

"He'll be all right. It's just a bump on the head. I'm the one who needs the stitches."

When they arrived at the emergency entrance to Groote Schuur Hospital, Levi was taken in one direction, Gary Martin in another. A little later the doctor on duty took Jay and Jenny into his office.

"What happened, Mrs. Bam?"

"There was an accident. Levi hit his head against the corner of the table. He fell and then didn't move."

"Does Levi have any allergies?"

"No, except for butter. He can't eat butter."

"Has he ever been hurt before?"

Jenny hesitated. "What do you mean?"

"Has he ever been hospitalized?"

"No, but he's very accident-prone. He's forever falling, bumping against corners. Small injuries, bruises, you know." She added hurriedly, "Levi is on Ritalin, Doctor. He's a hyperactive child."

"He's on no other medication?"

"No. Doctor, is he going to be okay?"

"Mrs. Bam, it could be serious. We'll let you know as soon as we know something for certain."

The doctor stood up and ushered Jenny and Jay out of his office.

"How can it be serious, Jay? It was only a bump on the head."

Jenny was crying. Black rivulets were running down her cheeks. Jay fetched some tissues, and she tried to wipe off the mascara smears.

"He didn't mean to hit him so hard. Gary doesn't know how to deal with kids—and neither do I," she sobbed.

"Jenny, it'll be all right. He'll be fine," Jay said. A sense of helplessness had overcome him.

One minute unpacking the Ark, tired, looking forward to my bed, a cup of hot chocolate, and an early night. The next, sitting in a hospital waiting for a verdict on a life. Where did this come from?

After an hour another doctor came into the room and introduced himself as the neurosurgeon. He asked Jenny to sign forms consenting to his operating on her son. In a daze Jenny signed the forms, while Jay watched without comprehending.

I've got a bad feeling. Levi, you've got to get well. God make Levi well. God make him well.

Time dragged by. Jay phoned his mother to tell her what had happened.

"Do you know a Mr. Gary Martin?" A young nurse stood before them with a clipboard in her hand.

"Yes, we know him," Jay answered when Jenny didn't.

"I just wanted to tell you we'll be admitting him for a few days. We need to keep him under observation for a while."

Way to go, Levi! Stick the bastard, make him bleed.

"Thank you," said Jay. "Jenny, don't you have to phone anyone?"

"No, but you don't need to stay with me, Jay. I'll let you know as soon as I hear."

"I want to stay, if you don't mind. I don't know how it happened, but somehow Levi has become my closest friend."

"He needs friends. It hasn't been easy, Jay, his not having a father."

Tell me about it.

Judgments and accusations floated in Jay's mind, but he fought against uttering them.

It's too easy to look in from the outside and know everything.

The night wore on. Nurses hurried by, patients were rolled in and out on stretchers, and a sense of fear, pain, and illness permeated everything.

I hate hospitals. Look at that woman sitting in front of her typewriter, answering the phone, checking her order form. How can she be so placid when we are sitting here waiting for a verdict?

At last they saw the neurosurgeon come through the swinging door at the end of the passage. Jenny and Jay went to meet him.

Tell us he's fine. Don't make us walk all that way. Shout good news from where you are.

There was nowhere else to look but at each other. The surgeon's face was blank. He walked the last few meters searching abstractedly for something in his pockets.

"I'm very sorry, Mrs. Bam. Levi died a few minutes ago."

"God, no!"

"Levi had suffered a depressed skull fracture—"

"But he just banged his head . . ."

"The fracture caused bleeding in the brain, and we couldn't control it. We did everything we could, but Levi never regained consciousness. It was a very bad injury. I'm very sorry."

Somewhere in the last words Jay sensed a question, but when he looked more closely at the surgeon's face he thought he must have been mistaken. Jenny clung to Jay and wept. She gripped his shoulder so hard that he winced.

Levi dead. Lee the stoic, nine-year-old kid with an attitude— gone.

163

"I want to go home," sobbed Jenny.

Jay gently turned her around and took her out of the hospital. It was night outside, and there was hardly any traffic. Everything seemed obscenely normal to Jay. He didn't know what to do with the anger rising in him.

You knew it was coming, you little sod! That's why you came with us. You knew it was coming. It was your final voyage. That's why you wanted to go with Carol. You knew she was your last chance—the only way you could avoid this. Was life at home so horrible, old man, that you wanted no part of it? This is crazy, Jay-o. It was an accident! Accidents happen. How could he have known?

Jay drove Jenny home, parked the truck outside the cottage, and waited while she opened the front door.

"Do you want me to come in?"

"No. I need to be alone. Thank you for everything you've done tonight. I don't know what I would have done without you."

Jay turned and left the Bam cottage. He walked across Darien Square and up Station Road. Only when he had reached the top of the road did he realize where he was headed. He crossed the road and contemplated the looming yellow-washed presence of Groote Schuur Hospital, where he had spent the last few miserable hours. Without caring who might see, he opened the flap in the cemetery fence and climbed through the hole. He walked between the graves until he found the small stone statue of the boy holding a cat.

Only when he sat down at the foot of the statue did he start to weep.

TRANSFORMATIONS

"I will build a home on Smokey Hill, and it will shine like a beacon for every poor soul in the district. The walls will be solid, the roof will be sound, and on the table there will always be hot soup and fresh bread. That's my dream." The woman smiled. The dream would finally be realized. She would find the children—homeless, handicapped, abandoned, children needy in whatever way—and she would build them a home . . .

THE WRITING TRAILED OFF, and Jay searched through the other papers to find the conclusion to Chuck's story. Disappointed, he put the story down and ticked off an item on the list he was compiling of his grandfather's papers. He was sitting in his loft bedroom with his grandfather's box open before him on the floor and piles of papers scattered about him. He was methodically sorting the documents contained in the box and had discovered that they had been organized according to a system: Each document had been numbered and dated to form part of a sequence. When he'd first opened the box at Klasie's he had inadvertently disturbed that sequence, but he was now getting everything back in order again.

Not bad, Gramps. Not great on finishing, but a good turn of phrase, and you certainly knew how to weave an intricate plot line.

Jay picked up another paper and started to read. At first he had struggled to decipher Chuck's spidery handwriting, but once he had gotten used to it he had been able to read without too much difficulty.

Levi wanted to stay at Eventide. He would have loved this story.

It was four days since the boy had died. During that time Jay had been in a daze. With the shock still fresh he had found the days dragging endlessly between the time he woke and the time he went to sleep again. He had found no solace with any of his new friends. His mother had been eager with questions, which he had only half answered or had shrugged off entirely. For the first time, ironically, he had had a lucid conversation with his grandmother, who had quizzed him vigorously about his journey. When he had told her everything she had wanted to know, she had slipped back into her private world, satisfied.

Eventually he had had to find something to do. He could no longer endure his lethargy. He had succumbed to the lure of his grandfather's box and had begun to explore its contents.

And what an exploration it was turning out to be! The box contained letters to Chuck from May; 181 short stories, each neatly stapled together; 6 chapters of an aborted novel; a folder of 98 poems; 65 pieces of prose; a plastic folder of legal documents; two attempts at the first act of a play; a small leather book with an index of each piece of writing, recording where and when it had been written; a scrapbook of newspaper clippings; a dictionary and a thesaurus; a pencil box with a sharpener, eraser, and paper clips; and, what for Jay was the most exciting find of all, 12 black books containing journal entries dating back to 1945.

The more he read, the more his grandfather took shape as someone deeply unsure of his skill as a writer and extremely self-conscious about what he thought of as his amateurish attempts at fiction. Jay could see why his grandfather had had doubts about his writing ability. The occasional flash of brilliance did not compensate for the mostly banal, uninspired meandering in his early pieces from the mid-eighties, but as Jay worked through to his grandfather's more recent stories he noticed an improvement both in style and content. He was impressed, too, by the meticulous way his grandfather had dated, numbered, and listed each piece of his output. The man had obviously taken pride in organizing his work for easy reference. It would take Jay several weeks to read all the material his grandfather had produced in his lifetime.

Everything I always wanted to know about you, your life, what you thought, what you felt, what you believed, is here, Chuck. You knew that when you left me this treasure. And now I understand.

No longer did Jay feel the bitter disappointment that had assailed him when he had first opened the box. Though puzzled as to why so much of the writing had been left unfinished, he was amazed at what the box contained. It had turned out to be a treasure chest: the work of an unpublished but dedicated writer.

"Hardback, Klasie, the way real writers publish." A good dream to have, I suppose.

Some of the stories rushed along at a cracking pace, only to peter out. Others ended in mid-sentence as if the writer had been interrupted at his work. The poems were complete but tedious. Jay enjoyed the short stories most; even if they were unpolished and often no more than sketches of an idea, he could imagine his grandfather writing them, and he recognized characters and settings from Chuck's life. There was a comic story about the sale of a cement-stuffed elephant to Mr. Boswell of the Boswell Wilkie Circus. Another story dealt with the writer's journey up to Swakopmund, his meeting with a German diamond digger, and their brush with the South African police as they smuggled a packet of diamonds onto a freighter. Another story focused on a family named Van Dijk on a sheep farm in the karoo. It was a disturbing story about an intimate relationship between the owner of the farm and a black woman who worked for him.

Jay had just stretched out to continue reading this story when he heard his mother coming up the stairs.

What now? Can't she just leave me alone?

There came a tap on the door and Margaret's voice calling his name. Jay sprang up and opened the door a crack.

"Jason, there are two policemen downstairs. They want to talk to you." Margaret's voice was strained. "I think they want to ask you some questions about Levi."

It had to happen, I suppose. I was expecting this. What do I say about your falls and collisions with doorknobs and sharp corners, old man?

"I'm coming. Just a moment."

Jay waited for his mother to go downstairs again before he closed the door, but she hovered, peering over his shoulder at the papers on the floor.

"Are those all Chuck's? What are they?" she asked.

"Ma, please, I told you, they're only old papers, nothing very interesting. I'll let you see them when I've finished."

"All right, Jason. Whatever you say." Margaret turned and walked away, hurt by her son's exasperated tone.

Jay hurriedly tidied his hair and then went down to the policemen, one in plainclothes and the other in uniform, who were waiting in the living room.

They all sat down, and the plainclothes man, Detective Johnson, began asking Jay questions about Levi. Jay responded with answers that quickly made him realize how little he had known about the boy. The uniformed detective questioned him about Jenny Bam, and there, too, Jay could give little information.

"You say you noticed that the boy was often bruised and that recently he had a black eye?"

Jay was becoming increasingly uncomfortable as he realized the direction their questioning was taking.

"Yes, a couple of weeks ago Levi did have a black eye. He said he had fallen off the table or something. He was always bumping into things. He seemed to be accident-prone."

"That was what his mother said," Detective Johnson replied.

Why do I want to defend Jenny? Why do I feel like an accomplice? Yes, I knew there was something strange about your bruises, and I did nothing about them.

"Another time Levi came to Bob Lo's hatchery—"

"Bob Lo?"

"I have a Saturday job at the Tropical Fish Emporium around the corner from where Levi lived. Anyway, one day he pitched up with a nosebleed. He said he had had an argument with Gary Martin."

"Mr. Martin had struck the boy?"

"Yes. On the face."

The policeman wrote down this information and then looked at Jay. "Now could you tell me what happened the day of the accident?"

Jay took a deep breath and ran his hand through his hair. He began recounting the events that had eventually led him and Levi up the path to the Bam cottage the day the boy had been injured. He told of his search for the box, how Levi had become involved, and how the boy had, without permission, gone on the journey to Knysna.

Finally he got to that Wednesday afternoon when he and Levi had reluctantly returned to Bam cottage. Now he spoke in short bursts as he tried to recall every detail.

Every now and then the detective would interrupt him with a question. He paid particular attention when Jay said, "I think Jenny and Gary had planned to punish Levi—he'd trashed Gary's tapes—by locking him in his room all day Monday while they went sailing. I remember Gary saying they hadn't discovered Levi was gone until very late Monday night. I'd left a message with my mother when I got no answer to my call on Monday night to tell Jenny what we'd decided to do."

After some questions about Gary Martin, none of which Jay was able to answer satisfactorily, the policeman asked Jay to make a written statement, thanked him, and left.

"It's terrible. I don't know what I would do if anything like that were to happen to you, Jay," Margaret said, coming back into the living room after showing the policemen to the door. Jay glanced at his mother and saw she was genuinely distressed. "I can't imagine what that poor woman must be going through."

"I'm going up to my room," he said.

"Jason . . ."

Margaret hesitated as he waited for her to speak. She hesitated even longer as she met her son's gaze, but continued, "It wasn't your fault, Jason. You didn't know he hadn't been given permission to go with you, and you did the right thing by going in with him to explain everything to his mother. You mustn't blame yourself."

"I don't, Ma. I just wish none of it had happened," Jay said miserably. He turned and went up to his room.

Once again the contents of the box were able to soothe Jay. He returned to discovering more about the journeys his grandfather had described with such care. As he read, he could imagine his grandfather traveling through the South African countryside, meeting people, talking to other travelers, and trying to find some way of bringing his life to a meaningful close.

Jay chose another story and spent the afternoon reading, until his eyes tired of the black spider scrawl and he decided he had read enough for the day. He was packing the papers neatly into the box when he again came across the folder of legal documents. He glanced idly through bank statements, check stubs, and records of mortgage repayments, then noticed a ten-page official-looking document. He flicked through its pages; at the bottom of each page he saw the signatures of his grandfather, his father, his uncle, someone he didn't know, and—surprisingly—Bob Lo.

He checked the date: The document was dated ten years ago.

Exactly when Chuck took off.

He began to read it. It seemed to be about a trust that had been set up by Chuck Watson. Jay scanned the first page, and then, as he turned to the second, he caught sight of his own name.

He read on more carefully.

In my absence I give Peter Hodges, my elder son, control over 32 percent of the assets in the Watson Pet Emporiums, namely 32 percent of the stock of all the Watson Pet branches, the cattle markets, the tropical fish outlets, and the granary depots. To Jack Watson, my younger son, I give control over 28 percent of the assets in the Watson Pet Emporiums, provided he continues to work as regional manager and distributing agent. The remainder of the stock, namely 40 percent, is to be held in trust, its income to be reinvested only in the Watson Pet Emporiums, and in no other business venture whatsoever. Peter Hodges shall administer this trust. At the age of eighteen, Jason Watson, my only grandson, shall take over full title to the 40 percent of the stock which shall have been held in trust for him.

I am to be given the lion's share in the Watson pet empire? Why hasn't anyone told me?

The rest of the document spelled out the details of what had been summarized on the second page. What puzzled Jay was that Bob Lo had also signed at the bottom of each page.

So you knew about this, Bob Lo, but you didn't tell me.

Jay's mind raced as he tried to sort out what he knew about the complexities of the Watson business. He had never before wondered how the adults in his life earned the money that he used so unthinkingly. He knew his father had hated his work. He had always made that very clear. He was a regional manager of the Watson Pet Emporiums, and he didn't even like animals. He had made many attempts to get away from Chuck's business and do something else. Time and again he had returned and had resumed work at the Emporiums. Jay knew very little about his uncle's involvement with the Emporiums. He seemed to have been only a silent partner in the whole affair. When the creditors started baying, Uncle Peter had not come to their assistance. In fact, he was out of the country when things became really unpleasant. Jay did, however, remember his father's complaining about his half brother's lack of interest in the Watson empire.

What Jay found hardest to assimilate were the implications of his grandfather's having made provision for him in the trust, despite how young Jay had been at the time.

I was only seven when he left, but he thought I had it in me to collect forty percent of the business when I was eighteen. What was he thinking?

A rush of excitement thrummed through Jay as hundreds of questions flooded his mind.

What is left of the Watson empire? And how much is forty percent of the stock worth? If Uncle Peter is administrator of the trust, what has he done with Chuck Watson's money? Is that why the Pumpkin Eater knew I would be coming to challenge him? And Bob Lo signed as a witness!

Hurriedly he packed away the rest of the papers, locked the box, shoved it under his bed, and, with the legal document in his hand, rushed downstairs.

"Jason? Are you all right?" Margaret called as her son dashed past her.

"Fine, I'm just fine. I'm going to the hatchery. Keep my supper for me—please!"

Jay ran out of the house and down Gordon Road to the Topical Fish Emporium.

Bob Lo was carrying a fish tank into his office. Before Jay could say anything, Bob Lo spoke, beaming at him. "Jay, I've found it! I knew that first attempt was going to lead somewhere. And it has!"

Bob Lo's eyes were shining as he put the fish tank down. Jay looked around the office in amazement. Everything had been tidied up: All the surfaces were clear; the papers on Bob Lo's desk had been piled neatly to one side; the feeding nets and knitting needles had all been put in jars, which stood in a neat row on the shelf. The microscopes had been covered. The office was immaculate.

"What's going on?"

"I've got it, Jason! A new species!" Bob Lo pointed proudly at two very small goldfish swimming around in the tank. "There they are! They hatched last week and I've examined them and they're perfect. Everything is correct—the heart-shaped scales, the dimensions, everything! Look at their color."

Bob Lo went rattling on, but all Jay could see in the tank were two seemingly ordinary goldfish.

Bob, you've finally gone off the tracks. They're just goldfish. That's all.

"That's great, Bob," Jay said, trying to work up some enthusiasm for what Bob Lo perceived as the pinnacle of his life's work.

"Great! It's more than great. It's bloody marvelous!" Bob Lo crowed triumphantly.

"Bob, I want to ask you something."

174

"Anything, Jay, anything. You want a raise? You've got it. These little beauties are going to become celebrities."

"No, I don't want a raise. I want to ask you about this."

Jay handed his grandfather's document to Bob Lo, who adjusted his glasses, read the front page, and looked quickly up at Jay.

"You found this in Chuck's box?"

"Yes. Your signature's on every page."

Bob Lo slowly sat down at his desk as he skimmed through the document.

"Ten years ago, huh?"

"Why didn't you tell me there was a trust waiting for me when I turn eighteen?"

"There is? I didn't know that. I never read this document, you know. Your grandfather was fed up, and he was planning to leave. He wanted me there to witness his signature. I signed lots of stuff as a witness. I didn't read any of it."

"What does it mean, Bob? There's something in there about me getting forty percent of the stock of the family business when I turn eighteen. That's only four months away."

"Will you shush for a minute and let me read it properly? Go inside and make yourself busy. The king khoi need to be fed, and the snout-nosed elephant couple's tank needs to be cleaned," Bob Lo said, dismissing Jay.

Jay wandered aimlessly through the hatchery. It was an overcast day, and the interior was dim; it smelled of stale water and dead fish, and felt clammy. He stopped in front of the king khoi tank and stared into its watery depths. A moonlight gourami swam idly by and blinked at Jay.

Hi, there, Princess, what's up? Stop. This talking to fish is dumb.

Jay threw some feed into the tank and walked away. He scooped out the snout-nosed elephant couple from their

175

tank, poured its water down the drain, refilled the tank, and casually threw the fish back into it. He didn't bother to clean the algae off the tank's sides. Instead, he merely tossed in a few monkey ferns and some clean sand. The chores could not hold his attention. He picked up a magazine and tried to read until Bob Lo was ready to talk to him. Fifteen minutes later Bob Lo called him into his office.

"It's really quite simple, Jay. Your grandfather has set up a trust of forty percent of the Watson family business. The trust will come to you when you turn eighteen. Your uncle was made the administrator of the trust, which means he must administer the funds in the best interest of the Watson business."

"But the business is on its knees. We long ago stopped getting any income from the Watson pet shops."

"I don't know anything about the financial side. You'll have to go see your uncle about that, but this document means that when you turn eighteen you will gain control over a large part of the stock of your grandfather's business."

I knew another visit to Camps Bay was coming up.

"Jason?"

"I have to go and see Uncle Peter again."

"It looks like it. He has a lot of explaining to do. It says here quite clearly that the money must be reinvested only in the Watson business. You must find out what happened to that money."

The flickering blue of an aquarium. "You see, Jason, I know why you are here: You've come to challenge me." He thought I knew about the trust.

Jay stood up, picked up the document that lay on Bob Lo's desk, and walked resolutely out of the office. As he reached the door Bob Lo called after him, "Good luck, Jason."

"I don't need any luck, Bob. I'm going to get what's rightfully mine."

Jay raised the fist-shaped knocker and banged it down loudly on the oak door. He waited a moment and then knocked again hard. The door was opened by a different black woman.

"Can I help you?"

"I've come to see Peter Hodges. He knows I'm coming. Tell him it's his nephew, Jason Watson.

"Won't you come in, Mr. Watson," the woman said pleasantly, opening the door wider for Jay to step into the entrance hall.

"I'll sit over here," Jay said, walking over to the aluminum chair next to the glass-topped table. He put his grandfather's box on the glass table, but when it creaked and wobbled he moved the box to the floor.

Artsy-fartsy furniture which fails dismally at being a table. And this artsy chair isn't much good either.

He shifted his foot to prevent himself from sliding forward on the slippery seat of the chair. He looked around at the decor that had previously so impressed him. Everything had been so fashionably selected it failed to make a home. When the woman had disappeared up the staircase he stood up and glanced through the sitting room door. The fish tank still shimmered in its blue neon light. He was not going to again risk being caught unawares by his uncle, and so he returned to his seat.

Peter Hodges appeared at the top of the staircase and, leaning over the balustrade, looked down at Jay. "Well, well, this is a surprise. It's the triumphant hero returning from his adventures." He came down the stairs and eyed the yellowwood box at Jay's feet. "So you found what you were looking for."

"Hello, Peter," Jay said, standing up to face his uncle.

"Hello, Jason. It's good to see you again. Would you like a drink?"

"No, thank you," Jay said curtly.

"Ah, I see. This is a business call, is it?" Peter smiled slightly at the solemnity of the young man standing before him.

You can't toy with me, Peter. I have an ace up my sleeve this time, which trumps your moon card.

"You could call it that."

"Well then, let's get on with it. Come with me to my study."

Jay followed his uncle up the staircase and down a carpeted corridor into his study. On one wall of the room was a wooden fixture whose shelves held a liquor cabinet, a television set, a VHS recorder, and a hi-fi stereo and compact disk system. Facing the open window, which looked out onto the ocean, was a large glass-topped desk. Behind the desk hung a vividly colored abstract painting, which to Jay looked like children's art.

Peter Hodges sat down in one of the two leather chairs facing the desk, indicating that Jay should take the other. Jay put the box at his feet.

"So Arthur Jacobs did have Chuck's precious box?"

"No, he didn't. I had to go through several other people before I found it."

"Oh yes? How fascinating."

"I went first to Mossel Bay, and then we drove up the coast and finally found it near Knysna."

"So you met that old drunk, Klasie. I should have guessed the box would probably have landed up with that old reprobate. I learned my first swearwords from Klasie. He's quite a character, isn't he?"

178

Jay nodded.

"So you've been on a journey." Peter Hodges formed a steeple with his fingers and looked benevolently over at Jay. "Your choice of the moon card was appropriate, after all. Has the goddess of the moon shed any light on your voyage, Jason? Were the contents of the box worth the chase?"

"I think they were. I found out something from them I never knew before."

Jason bent to take the trust document out of the box. He paused, as he phrased the question he hoped would floor Peter Hodges.

"Why was I never informed about the trust fund Chuck Watson had set up for me?" He handed the document to his uncle.

Glancing without interest at the document, Peter Hodges replied smoothly, "Because nobody thought you were old enough to understand what a trust fund was. You would have been told this year when you turned eighteen. It's not a big secret that we're all conspiring to keep from you. Not that you're going to get anything from it anyway."

"What do you mean?"

"Well, the way your father—no offense intended, Jason—ran his part of the business was, how should I put it, pretty inept. He made quite a few foolish mistakes—"

"But you control most of the stock."

"Yes, well, I'm afraid we have the economy of dear old South Africa to blame for the rest of the disaster. You can't have been so engrossed in your adolescence not to have noticed the way things have been going, economically speaking, in this country over the last ten years. You've heard about the economic sanctions and the ban on foreign trade, I trust? That meant that the bottom fell out of our export market. And then, of course, with the State of Emergency being declared the stock market took another dive. The renewed violence scared off more international investors. Over the last few years most South African businesses have taken quite a knock. Many have gone under entirely. I'm afraid quite a few of your grandfather's initial investments were not as sound as he thought they were."

Peter Hodges went on speaking confidently, elaborating on details he felt were pertinent. Jay felt his confidence draining away in the face of his uncle's equanimity.

"So how much will my stock be worth?"

Peter Hodges crossed his arms, sighed, and looked steadily at Jay. Although he kept his face carefully blank, his eyes held a flicker of amusement. "Nothing, I'm afraid."

He got up and went to his desk. He opened a drawer and pulled out a stack of papers, which he dumped on his desk.

"You see, Jason, everything's been lost because of the poor investments your grandfather made. Of course, your father didn't help matters much—"

"Just leave my father out of this!" Jay said angrily, feeling his temper flare in the face of Peter Hodges's cool assumption of superiority.

"But I'm afraid we can't leave him out of it, Jason. He made several illegal withdrawals from the trust fund. I didn't want to do anything about it, you know, his being family and all that, but he's as much to blame as anyone. Here are the bank statements over the last five years to substantiate my point. I'm afraid everything's been frittered away."

A depression settled on Jay as he listened to his challenge being so effectively undermined by his uncle's fluent account of the failure of the family business.

"Now, let's have a look at Chuck Watson's contribution. Chuck wanted to escape from the wicked life he was living as a white South African in an immoral society," Peter Hodges continued sardonically. "He no longer wanted to be a part of the, quote, exploitative, privileged class, unquote, and all of that rubbish. Well, liberal ideas are all very well and good, but they don't mix with business. Business is not concerned with morals. Did Chuck think that divesting himself of his responsibility would make him less privileged? Can a leopard change its spots?"

Jumping ahead, moving too fast on to other issues. Slow down, Uncle, I'm not following.

"But the business had been doing well. Grandfather had created an empire."

"Oh yes, but that was a long time ago. Look, let's face it, Jason, your father was never interested in animals, and neither was I. I wasn't going to spend my life selling rabbits and budgies. It might have been good enough for Chuck—"

"But lack of interest is no reason for throwing away a perfectly good business."

"Circumstances, Jason, not lack of interest. Think of the situation in this country. As I said before, times were changing. And a rather foolish business partner didn't help either."

Once again Jason flushed, but before he could retaliate Peter Hodges continued. "Look, I'll give you all these company books and documents. You can see for yourself."

He pushed the pile of papers and ledgers on his desk across to Jay, together with the document that Jay had so triumphantly handed him.

"Really, Chuck Watson's idealism was a little nauseating, don't you think?"

Jay didn't answer as he replaced the trust document in the box. He preferred not to tell Peter Hodges anything about his grandfather's involvement with Eventide. He felt his uncle's cynicism would smirch Chuck's efforts.

Under the onslaught of his uncle's words Jay was defenseless and sat in silence, feeling inarticulate frustration welling up inside him. What had he expected? That the Pumpkin Eater would fall on his knees and grovel at his feet asking for forgiveness?

After touching on various other family matters, Peter Hodges edged Jay out of his office and down the stairs. Before he knew it, Jay was standing in the hallway facing an open door.

"I would really like to talk to you some more," said his uncle, "but I'm rather busy at the moment. You must come back some other time and tell me about your adventures in tracking down the old box. They must have been quite fascinating."

"I'll do that," Jay said, defeated by his uncle's urbanity.

"I'm truly sorry that you came all this way for nothing, but it's given us another opportunity to talk to each other, hasn't it? I want to be friends with you, Jason. I'd like you to come around more often. Come for dinner one evening, and I'll introduce you to some of my friends. It would be fun," Peter Hodges said, resting his hand confidently on Jay's shoulder.

Jay nodded and, finding nothing to say, went out the door, the box under one arm, the bundle of papers and books his uncle had given him under the other.

"Oh, and give my love to your mother. Margaret's a very special woman. Good-bye, Jason, don't stay a stranger," Peter Hodges called as Jay walked despondently down the steps onto Camps Bay Drive. He didn't look back up at the house, but walked without thinking to the beach. His burdens were becoming increasingly heavy and awkward as he struggled through the thick sand toward the rocks.

I should throw all this junk into the sea. Everything. Let it all float away.

Instead, however, he sat down on the rocks, dumping the bundle from his uncle on one side of him, the box on the other. He gazed out at the tranquil line of the horizon and followed the flight of a seagull as it dipped and floated over Camps Bay Beach. Jay was hot and thought about swimming, but something held him back from the water.

He looked down at the casket beside him. Automatically he opened it: Just a short while before, its contents had seemed almost magical to him. He sighed and was about to close it again when the title of the story lying on top caught his eye: "Betrayal on a Tuesday Afternoon." It was a story that, somehow, up to now he had missed.

He picked up the sheaf of papers, and from its thickness he guessed it to be one of Chuck's more sustained efforts. He read the first sentence: *The worst kind of betrayal is that between brother and brother.* Intrigued, he read on.

Slowly he was drawn deeper into his grandfather's fiction. The beach and its attractions, the blue sky, the sound of the ocean, all faded. There was no lyrical flow to the narration, which progressed by a succession of staccato sentences. Words leapt out at him. The writer intended his point to be emphatically driven home.

The story was about two brothers, a woman, and a seven-year-old boy. The brothers worked in business together. The older brother was efficient, the younger was not. The older brother often visited his brother's wife.

Stop. Don't read on. The boy is thirsty. He wants a drink from the fridge. I spy with my little eye.

Jay read on.

The older brother climbed the stairs and entered the bedroom of his brother's wife.

The fridge is locked. He wants something cold to drink. He needs to fetch the key. His mother is asleep upstairs. He hears a noise.

The older brother kissed his brother's wife on the mouth. He stroked her hair, her shoulders, the small of her

183

back. She pulled him closer. The afternoon was hot. Outside, a warm berg wind blew.

Jay found he had trouble breathing. He rapidly scanned the next pages: He did not have to read what he already knew. The words rekindled images that pushed themselves to the forefront of his mind.

The boy climbs the stairs. His thirst is forgotten. What are the sounds coming from his mother's bedroom?

The couple were oblivious to the boy's eyes at the door.

I open the door. A naked woman is sitting on a chair in my mother's bedroom. Her back is toward me. I wonder who she is. She wears a floppy hat. Uncle Peter is standing in front of her. He is white-naked, eyes closed. The woman turns around. I can't move. She is my mother.

The boy cried out when he saw his uncle with his mother. He ran from the house.

They don't see me. I run downstairs. I pick up a Coke bottle, smash it against the wall. Then I smash another Coke bottle against the wall.

Jay was breathing heavily. Memory flooded back.

That evening at the dinner table Margaret had been dishing up slices of orange pumpkin to her husband, and seven-year-old Jay had chanted:

"Peter, Peter, Pumpkin Eater,
Kissed Mommy and was a cheater.
Put her in a pumpkin shell,
And then they took off all their clothes."

Jay had burst into tears, and Margaret's face had betrayed her.

Weeks later, Jay, listening to his mother and his father in one of their fights downstairs, had heard: "I'll stay, but only because of Jason."

Jay returned to Chuck's story. He had reached the last page, which had been written in a hurried scrawl. The story jolted to an abrupt close: three revolver shots.

Bang, bang, bang! So in his story Chuck killed them. It would have been simpler in real life too. All those pinpricks of pain came later. The routine slighting and the cruel allusions that followed my rhyme. And my forgetting. For me it had never happened.

Carefully Jay put the story back in the box. He remembered everything. He knew all the answers.

So when I turned sixteen you declared me of age, Father? You had done your duty by me, and you could leave. I was an adult and your responsibility toward me had ended. Rubbish!

He stood up angrily, picked up the box under one arm and the bundle of paper and books under the other, and struggled over the rocks and sand back to the road. The sun sank as he waited for a bus to take him back to Observatory. He glanced up at the mountain, running his eyes along the stacked houses, and tried to locate his uncle's mansion.

And afterward, did you just abandon Margaret, Peter? Three living in hatred and all because of a dirty rhyme.

The French windows of the white mansion flashed at Jay as he climbed aboard the bus.

We're not yet finished, Uncle.

Back in Observatory Jay ate the supper his mother had kept for him. Recognizing a new seriousness in her son, Margaret fussed over him. Jay responded warmly to her, and she was touched by his unusual gentleness. Jay watched her prepare his food and felt her sitting quietly across from him as he stared at the television without watching. He could no longer find it in him to blame her for that hot berg-wind afternoon.

Mother. That was it

He had thought of her only as the mother and necessary prop of his existence. Now for the first time he saw her as a woman, a person with her own needs.

We make mistakes. All of us. Big mistakes.

"Great supper, Margaret. Thanks," he said.

Margaret looked up, startled at her son's use of her first name.

"I'm glad you liked it, Jason. Will you have some more? There's plenty left."

"Yes, I would. Don't worry, I'll get it."

Jason got up, but his mother stood at the same time and took the tray from him. "No, you sit down. There's something in this evening's newspaper about Levi."

The second page carried a photograph of Levi Bam. The boy gazed somberly into the camera with his well-remembered expression.

You got your face into the papers, old man. I wish you hadn't.

Under the photograph, with a caption reading "Charges filed in Levi Bam accident," there was a paragraph about a pending case.

Today in the Cape Town Regional Court, Mr. Gary Martin of Woodstock was charged with culpable homicide following the death of a nine-year-old boy, Levi Bam. The boy's mother, Ms. Jenny Bam, was charged with being an accessory to the crime. A hospital spokesman from Groote Schuur Hospital has stated that there were both old and new bruises on Levi Bam when he was admitted to Groote Schuur on the night of the accident. Levi Bam suffered severe cerebral damage when he struck his head after stabbing Mr. Martin, his mother's lover. Mr. Martin has not yet been asked to plead, and Ms. Bam has refused to comment. The case will resume on 2 March.

What could she say: I beat my kid when he didn't listen, I let my macho boyfriend beat him too. That he needed a male role model, and so he made friends with a local kid who didn't pay much attention to him or his bruises?

"Did you know Levi was being treated so badly?" his mother asked as she gave Jay his food.

"No, I always thought his 'accidents' were those of a weird kid who had strange ideas about how to have fun."

"What do you think will happen to them?"

"I don't know. There's going to be a trial. I don't think it looks good."

"It wasn't very good for Levi, was it?"

"No, it wasn't. Where's Gran?" Jay asked, suddenly missing his grandmother from her usual place in front of the television.

"She's in her room. She's been spending a lot of time up there lately. She's been rummaging through some of Chuck's things, but I think it's harmless. Thank goodness she's finally lost her appetite for the silver," Margaret said. Despite himself, Jay had to laugh at the woeful expression on his mother's face. She laughed with him, pleased that something had relieved his gloom.

In the pause that followed an intolerable heaviness settled upon Jay.

Water. Get thee to the place of rainbows, light, and gliding, Jay-o. Wash away these Levi thoughts.

"Ma, I'm going over to Bob Lo's for a while."

"It's late, Jason."

"I know, but I won't be long."

Walking through the quiet evening streets to Bob Lo's, Jay ran through the day's events. He was slowly unwinding threads from the cocoon of the past. The recall of forbid-

187

den memory that afternoon had answered all the questions he had asked himself about his father, his family's relationship with Peter Hodges, and Chuck's attitude toward his sons. Jay murmured the rhyme over to himself: He remembered composing it lying on his bed staring up at the ceiling.

You calculating, self-righteous, vindictive little brat, Jay-o. Hurting your mother because you had decided she should be punished.

The old Victorian house at the end of Fish Alley was dark when Jay arrived. He called out for Bob Lo and was relieved to get no answer. He opened the gate, entered the house, and made his way to the office.

"Bob!" he called again. There was no reply.

He opened the metal door and wandered through the hatchery, dipping his hand into the tanks and enjoying the cool lick of water.

What real stories I have now! Not fantasy wisps of princesses and kings, but real, hurting, alive stories about people I know.

The hatchery was dark and warm, the purring of the water pumps soothing. Jay decided not to turn on the lights, because framed in the center of one of the skylights was a half-moon, its reflection flickering on the water's surface in the various tanks. As Jay stood watching the silvery shimmering, a feeling of security washed through him.

One more time.

Jay stripped off his shoes, socks, shirt, and denims, and, after a moment's hesitation, stepped out of his underpants as well. He went into the water naked. It was cooler than he had expected and he shivered slightly. The fish, watery shadows, flicked frantically up and down the sides of the tank as he settled to the bottom. He landed painfully on a rock and moved it out of the way to the side of the tank.

He hoped to revel in experiencing once again all the old sensations: the music of the water, the feather touch of fish, the ceaseless gurgling of the water pumps. But then, as the water settled above his head, the underwater world assumed a menacing aspect. Pale streaks of moonlight played upon the tanks around him. He looked up, and through the water he saw the moon's shimmer, a blurred slither of silver set in darkness.

Moon Slippery silver coin. When will I be free of her realm? Half-moon, a slice of shivery silver. Are you out there, Levi, sailing in the night sky? Is it a quiet, peaceful place with no corners or clenched fists?

The water was cold and brittle against Jay's skin; the rasping of his breathing was an eerie, disembodied sound. Water pushed in on him, and he felt the first stirring of claustrophobia. He shivered again. Something slid across his back: The sinewy length of an eel flicked silently past his face. In fright his head jerked back against the glass, and he choked on a slop of old water as the snorkel dipped momentarily beneath the surface. Another, larger shape sidled past him to sink into the dark corners of the tank.

Submerged, Jay heard nothing but his own rasping breath and the pumps' repetitive thuds. He tried to concentrate on recapturing the experiences he had previously enjoyed so effortlessly: Slowly he came to understand that the once-familiar fantasy world had gone forever. In its place was something dark and threatening.

He had to get out of the tank, out of the water. It was ridiculous to sit there shivering and gasping for breath. He could no longer make up fantasies when there was work to be done and a life to live.

Jay took hold of the sides and pulled himself out of the fish tank. Water surged across the floor. Spitting out his snorkel and choking on some excess water, he climbed out of the tank. He found his shoes and clothes, dressed, and walked down the length of the hatchery.

Good-bye, Princess Moonlight, Oscar, and King Khoi. You won't see me again.

He closed the heavy metal door and sat at his desk, staring at the old typewriter. A turmoil of thoughts and ideas were buzzing through his mind, but the idea that predominated was the one that focused on his uncle.

At the moment when he had arisen from the water, he had experienced a unique feeling, a revelation. He had known exactly what he was going to do. He would no longer hide in fish tanks, blowing bubbles and dreaming of rainbows. His grandfather had left him a legacy; he would claim what was rightfully his, and however that was to be done it had to start with the white mansion at Camps Bay, and Peter Hodges.

You offered me the chance to read your books and papers, Uncle. Tomorrow I'll do just that—with the help of an attorney. I can't take on my uncle by myself, and I don't have to. Uncle, I know you are lying: All I have to do is prove it. Tomorrow it will begin.

TEN DAYS LATER Jay and Sam Goldberg, the attorney recommended to him by Bob Lo, climbed the steps to 118 Campus Bay Drive. Jay carried a briefcase.

This time I'm wearing both my shoes, Peter Pumpkin Eater.

He stood in front of his uncle's door and looked at Sam Goldberg. "This is it," he said grimly.

"Well, knock, and let's get it over with," Sam said.

Jay raised the fist knocker and banged twice. This time Peter Hodges opened the door himself. He smiled at Jay and then saw Sam Goldberg.

"Right on time, Jason. I didn't know you were bringing someone with you."

"This is Mr. Sam Goldberg, my attorney."

Peter Hodges looked surprised, shrugged, and motioned them to go into his sitting room. They sat down on one of the couches. Peter Hodges offered them a drink.

"I don't think we want to waste time with drinks. We are here on business."

"Oh? And I thought this was a social call, Jason." Peter Hodges looked speculatively at Jay as he sat down opposite them. "What nasty little surprise have you got up your sleeve?"

"Mr. Goldberg and I have been going through the books you gave me. We have also investigated your business affairs and your ties with the Watson Emporiums through other sources. It seems you have used monies from the trust fund to start various subsidiary businesses. This goes against your father's stipulations. You siphoned money from the trust fund and invested the capital and the accumulated interest in your own businesses."

Jay took a paper out of the briefcase and placed it in front of his uncle. "In 1984 you formed the Hodges Company and used trust money to buy your first property. In 1987 you again used trust money to make investments in two unsound companies, which subsequently went bankrupt. Two years later Hodges, Incorporated, bought up these two companies, thus almost trebling your initial investment and, conveniently, showing the trust money to have been supposedly badly invested."

Peter Hodges did not raise his eyes from the papers Jay laid, one by one, before him. Jay spoke with confidence, calmly and steadily. Sam Goldberg sat quietly next to him, observing Peter Hodges.

"These were all legal transactions, Jason. I don't know where you got this information from, but it seems you have been misinformed," said Peter Hodges smoothly, glancing at the attorney.

"I don't think so." Sam Goldberg spoke for the first time. "We have proof here of your gross mishandling of the trust fund left in your charge by Chuck Watson."

"That's preposterous! Chuck Watson's business was on the bones of its backside, run by an incompetent ass who had no sense in his head," Peter Hodges said icily.

Jay considered his uncle gravely and laid another sheet of paper before him. "Fraudulent administration of a trust fund is a criminal offense. I intend to turn the files over to the public prosecutor and bring a criminal action against you."

Peter Hodges, apparently impassive, met his nephew's glance, but Jay had seen shock flicker across his uncle's eyes.

"We intend to bring a civil suit against you for the monies you secretly invested, for a percentage of the profits of those investments, for a share in the properties and businesses you purchased, and for the loss consequent upon the Watson empire's depleted earning power," Sam Goldberg said.

"What! You can't be serious. They'll throw you out of court." Peter Hodges spoke angrily and stood up to move away from the couches. Behind his back Jay glanced at Sam, who winked at him.

When Peter Hodges turned back he was composed. He concentrated on Jay, ignoring the attorney. "You and I know you can't get away with this in a court. It will take years to sort out, and you can't afford lawyers' fees. You do realize that that man beside you will bleed you of every cent?"

"We are confident of winning, Mr. Hodges. It's you who will be paying my fee," Sam Goldberg said.

Peter Hodges did not answer the attorney. He strolled over to the aquarium, where he considered the fish for a while before he came to a decision. He swung around abruptly. "I'm prepared to consider a settlement."

"We're not interested in a settlement."

"Jason, you should at least hear what he has to say," Sam demurred.

"No, Sam. That's not good enough. I've found out how you became rich, Peter, and I'm not going to allow you to get away with it. I know what I have to do: If it means going to court, then I'll go to court. And anyway, it's more than just a question of money."

Peter Hodges contemplated Jay and came back to the glass-topped table. He sat down. "Oh, so you finally know, do you?"

"Yes, there was a great deal in that yellowwood box."

"Ahh, so that's it! You want to punish me for my indiscretion?"

"No, what occurred between you and my parents happened a long time ago. It's none of my business. All I'm interested in now is getting what is due to me, and finishing something Chuck started and was unable to finish."

Jay and Sam Goldberg gathered up their belongings and left the baffled Peter Hodges planning his strategy.

Once back in his car, Sam Goldberg turned to Jay and grinned. "We've got him rattled."

"How can you tell? He seemed confident."

"Oh no, he wasn't. He was sweating on the top line. I think you shook him. But it's not going to be easy, Jason. It's not the first time he'll be in court."

"We have to make him pay up, Sam. We have to win."

"We will. Of that I have no doubt. By the time we've finished with him, you'll be quite a wealthy young man, Jason."

"The money's not all for me. There's a woman in Mossel Bay who will get a large part of it. What's the next move?"

"Well, we'll give him a couple of days to stew in his own juice and see if he comes up with a counterproposal. And then we slap him with a lawsuit that will give him nightmares and will need a team of lawyers to sort out. To put it bluntly, Jason, we've got your uncle by the short and curlies!"

I've achieved something. I've set wheels in motion. Nothing will stop me now.

Jay asked to be dropped off on the main road. As he got out of the car he found he was facing the Groote Schuur Cemetery, looking straight at the stone statue of David Leviticus Howard, who held a cat and stared out at the passing world.

I've done it. Levi, why aren't you here to celebrate with me? I'd take you for an ice cream and we'd watch trains together.

Jay turned and walked down Station Road toward his home. He passed the deserted lot. The letters GH-MK were still painted on the white wall. He stopped in front of the wall and stared at the letters.

194

GH-MK? Where have I seen those letters before?

The image of his grandfather scribbling something on a piece of paper snapped into Jay's mind. He remembered his grandfather looking at him urgently and jabbing at him with his forefinger. He remembered puzzling over the paper, being unable to decipher its scrawl, and then putting it away in a drawer.

Jay quickened his pace. He entered their house just as his grandmother came down the stairs. She was dressed in a man's dark suit, had a tie knotted around the loose folds of her neck, and her hair was neatly rolled up behind her head. She carried a briefcase.

"Hello, Granny," Jay said as he passed her on the staircase. "Where are you going?"

"None of your business, Jason."

As she came out of the kitchen Margaret caught sight of her mother-in-law, gasped, and then groaned loudly.

"Jason, please come and help me with Nana."

"What's the matter now?" the old woman said irritably. "It's only clothes I'm wearing. I'm not doing anyone any harm."

So Gran has given up silver spoons and is into cross-dressing now. Some things don't change in the Watson household!

"I'm tired of being an old woman. I want to be an old man for a change. Chuck always seemed to get a lot of fun out of it. I want to see what it feels like. Now, stop fussing, Margaret."

Oh, what to do with the spoon-swallowing Gran, who wants to be a man!

"You just can't go outside like that, Nana. Promise me you won't go outside," Margaret pleaded.

Jay left them arguing in the sitting room and went up to his room. He scuffled in his chest of drawers, praying he

195

hadn't lost the last piece of writing his grandfather had personally handed to him. At the back of a drawer he found the piece of paper. The scrawl was shaky, but now he could see there was no mistaking the letters: *GH-MK*.

Turn again to the yellowwood box for answers, Jay-o. Everything you need to know lies there.

Jay opened the box and searched for his grandfather's black index book. He turned over its pages: On the last page he found the letters *GH-MK*. It was the code for one of the last stories Chuck had written.

Jay looked through the papers and found the story. His grandfather had titled it "The Genuine Half-Moon Kid." Intrigued, Jay threw himself down on his bed and started reading.

It was about a grandfather and his grandson. It told how a grandfather loved his grandson but was unable to tell him so; how the old man, disappointed with the boy's parents, went away and so couldn't be with the boy; how one day the grandfather came back, but the boy, grown older, was reluctant to spend time with the old man; how slowly the grandfather and his grandson became friends.

Chuck was writing about the time he would have liked to spend with Jay. It could have been poignant, a story about lost opportunities, but on the last few pages the writing became absurdly sentimental and petered out. Like so many of Chuck's other stories it was incomplete.

An idea had slowly been forming in Jay's head. There was something he remembered in one of his grandfather's last journal entries. He pulled out the last volume and thumbed through its pages. He found the entry he was looking for:

> This writing business! If only I had started when I was young and foolish. How different my skill and discipline would be by now. If only I had jotted down those fantastic plots when I was young and passionate. My hardbacks

would be packing my shelves, but now the ideas and words come slowly, laboriously, and I can't finish, I can't finish . . .

The passage trailed off.

I will finish this story.

Jay leapt up and ran down the stairs. "Ma, I'm going over to Bob's. See you in a while."

When Jay arrived at the hatchery Bob Lo was hunched, as usual, over a tank of goldfish. He smiled when his assistant walked in.

"Jason, it's good to see you! Did you fight and slay your dragon?"

"I've just returned from Peter Hodges. It looks like it's going to be a long battle, but Sam Goldberg is confident we'll win."

"And you?"

"I am too. Peter Hodges didn't cover his tracks all that well, and we have a lot of proof."

"Good, good, I'm glad."

"Bob, I've come to tell you that I won't be working in the hatchery anymore. My life is going to get very busy for a while."

"I thought that might be the case. You're growing up, you bloody monkey. By the way, I've put some of your stuff over there." Bob Lo nodded at Jay's old desk.

"The typewriter isn't mine, Bob."

"It is now. I'm giving it to you. I can't use the bloody thing, so it's yours."

You read my mind, Bob.

"Thanks, Bob. That's great! Let me help you feed the fish one last time."

For several hours Bob and Jay worked together companionably, as they had done so often in the past. Finally, tired out, they called it a night, and Bob Lo accompanied Jay out through the house. When they got to the front gate, Jay turned to his friend.

"Bob, I've never told you before. I've really enjoyed working for you. I'm going to miss you."

"I'm going to miss you too. But the Topical Fish Emporium will always be here. So don't be a stranger."

"I won't. Goodnight, Bob, I'll see you again."

"You better!"

Jay walked jubilantly down Fish Alley, his typewriter under his arm and his head bubbling with words.

When he got home he climbed the stairs to his room, found a sheet of paper, and typed the title of Chuck's last story at the top of the blank page: "The Genuine Half-Moon Kid." He didn't know what the words meant, but they felt right. He was sure that once he started writing, their meaning would be revealed to him. He opened his grandfather's last journal to the entry he had read earlier that evening, and read the words again.

There's an answer here. Time—use it wisely. It doesn't matter what you do, as long as you do it with passion.

He reread his grandfather's version of "The Genuine Half-Moon Kid," and then, under the newly typed title on the clean sheet of paper waiting for him in his typewriter, he added: *A story dedicated to the memory of Levi Bam.*

With that he began typing.

As the story flowed onto the paper he saw Levi's face in his mind's eye. He was writing about a boy who had longed for a grandfather, and he gave Levi the grandfather whom the boy had never had—a wise, funny, gentle, eccentric old man who loved and valued his grandson. The words came rapidly, without effort; Jay could hardly type fast enough to keep up with his own creation.

Levi, I write this for you.

Jay wrote late into the night; he was still clicking away at his typewriter when Margaret turned off the lights and went to bed. As he typed, other stories intertwined with the main one: about Khayelitsha, and a woman who lived in a shoe with hundreds of children, and a woodcutter in the Knysna forest, and an old man driving through the countryside searching for South Africa.

As he typed, as the words flowed, Jay perceived the future opening up before him.

Hardback, Chuck's dream of hardback. Dream on, Jay-o. But why not? Start young, get ideas down . . .

And as he typed, so he took the first steps of his adult life. There he was, hair red and tangled as ever, hunched over the Corona, punching out his first story, words flooding his mind, images flashing from his fingers, everything coming easily to his young mind. He had found his passion.

Deep into the night Jay completed the last sentence of his first story, pulled the last sheet of paper from the typewriter, and added it to the neat stack of typed sheets. He stood up, opened the window, and looked out into the night. A half-moon slid out from behind a wisp of clouds.

Chuck, I have felt you around me. You're out there somewhere. A lost boy named Levi Bam is out there too. Find him. Take his hand. Take him home.

about the author

MICHAEL WILLIAMS grew up in South Africa. He has been a teacher in Kathmandu, Nepal, an assistant professor for New Sadler's Wells Opera in London, and a theater professor on board a ship for the University of Pittsburgh's Semester at Sea program. He is currently an opera producer for the Nico Theatre in Cape Town, South Africa. Mr. Williams has been active in bringing opera to schoolchildren in the townships, using his own compositions based on South African folklore.

The author's books include *Crocodile Burning*, an American Library Association Best Book for Young Adults, *Into the Valley*, and *My Father and I*.